The Heiress of Newfield

A Novel

by

Tina Appleton Bishop

iUniverse, Inc.
New York Bloomington

The Heiress of Newfield

Copyright © 2009 by Tina Appleton Bishop

All rights reserved. No part of this book may be used or reproduced by any means, graphic, electronic, or mechanical, including photocopying, recording, taping or by any information storage retrieval system without the written permission of the publisher except in the case of brief quotations embodied in critical articles and reviews.

iUniverse books may be ordered through booksellers or by contacting:

iUniverse
1663 Liberty Drive
Bloomington, IN 47403
www.iuniverse.com
1-800-Authors (1-800-288-4677)

Because of the dynamic nature of the Internet, any Web addresses or links contained in this book may have changed since publication and may no longer be valid. The views expressed in this work are solely those of the author and do not necessarily reflect the views of the publisher, and the publisher hereby disclaims any responsibility for them.

ISBN: 978-1-4401-8182-5 (sc)
ISBN: 978-1-4401-8183-2 (ebook)

Printed in the United States of America

iUniverse rev. date: 10/09/2009

To Myra

Author's Acknowledgements

Writing is a lonely job. A writer needs constant encouragement as well as stimulation. My membership in the Greenwich branch of the Pen Women of America provided this.

In addition one needs the patience and taste of a good editor. My younger son, Erik Hendricks, was a great help to me. I had always been warned against "doing business with family," and his suggestions caused me considerable re-writing, but his ideas were presented with such diplomacy that I had to concede that he was right.

My older son, Peter Hendricks, was also an important aid in producing this book. I am grateful to him for the photography and graphic design of the cover.

The response received from audiences at book talks on my first novel, "Fisherman's Creek," gave me the courage to attempt, at 91, another suspense novel. I suspect it will be my last book, but who knows!

1

Grieving

On a chilly, dismal day in October of 1968, the Eliot sisters stood trembling on the altar steps of the First Lutheran Church in Newfield, Connecticut. It was the saddest, most wretched day of their young lives: the memorial service for their father, Alfred Eliot, Jr., dead at 40 of a tragic fall in their landmark house, Eliot Farm.

Alberta and Fredrika (a composite of their father's name) or "Al" and "Freddie" as they inevitably would be called, were as unlike as any two girls could be. Freddie, at 18, had the red hair and the tall, awkward build of her father. Al, a blonde, already had, at 15, the signs of a voluptuous shape like her late mother, Mary Jane. Nevertheless, they were known to all as "The Boys."

Standing in similar – and equally unbecoming – black dresses, the girls tried, with shaking hands, to read excerpts from the service. It was as difficult for them to struggle through it as it was to watch them. Luckily, the ceremony was short, and the eulogies, too. After all, what can one say about a man who lived a dull, uneventful life, except that last, dramatic end? "He was kind, gentle and lovable" – and clumsy.

Tensely watching the two sisters, a stout, round faced, gray-haired woman sat alone in the front pew. Gretchen Downs had been a vital part of the Eliots' life ever since the death of Mary Jane, of a heart attack, 12 years ago. Soon after, she had been hired to take care of the house and the two little girls. They adored her. Alfred had never remarried. He didn't need to – he had Gretchen.

"You have a real jewel there in Gretchen," the neighbors told Alfred.

He agreed. She was, at 43, fifteen years older than he, and as uninterested in remarriage as he was. With Gretchen he felt safe, and under her watch the big Victorian house had never looked better. The three Eliots thrived. Her cooking skill was legendary, her pies and cakes featured at all of the Lutheran church suppers.

Mary Jane had been a gifted cook, too, and a remarkable silver polisher, floor waxer and window cleaner, but Gretchen surpassed her.

Alfred appreciated his good fortune. Gretchen's housekeeping, especially the high shine on the parquet floor of the front parlor – a room that was rarely used – always dazzled visitors to the house. The family preferred the former dining room next to it, which had been made into a cozy sitting room. Its floor was covered with a faded old braided rug, handmade by a past generation. The furnishings were comfortably shabby, except for a handsome, beautifully polished, drop-leaf dining table, which was used for occasional guests. In contrast to the formidable fieldstone fireplace in the front room, there was a cozy Franklin stove in one corner. Much as they loved that room, the girls preferred the huge, yellow-painted kitchen, where they would sit and watch Gretchen as she worked.

Originally, she had been hired as an "accommodator," a quaint word once used to describe ladies who were not servants (God forbid that you should consider them that!), but well-educated, capable women who were available for certain duties around the house. In the period after Mary Jane's death Gretchen worked a full day, and once in a while, until late at night. Then, a few weeks later, both Gretchen and Alfred decided that neither of them were gossip fodder, so she moved into the fifth bedroom, which was located on the top floor, next to the attic. The room was not large, but spacious enough for her big brass bed, her sturdy oak furniture, her precious old cuckoo clock and her collection of Bavarian china.

Much as he loved his children, it was a relief to him to have an occasional night out for dinner with neighbors or an evening at the movies. As the years passed, Alfred at forty remained a sought-after bachelor. His dark red hair had thinned a bit and his gait was as awkward as ever, but he had a sort of bashful charm that made him popular in the neighborhood. He was the poor woman's Gary Cooper, gawky but sweet. Dancing with him was a joke, however. Even he laughed at his clumsiness.

But who could have guessed that that very clumsiness would cost him his life?

After his memorial service Gretchen had sobbed, "It was my fault. I was much too proud about the high polish on that floor."

It seemed that Alfred had ordered some nice presents from Tiffany for the girls and was expecting a delivery. When he looked out of his bedroom window one morning and spotted the United Parcel truck, he quickly raced downstairs in order to intercept the packages before Alberta and Fredrika saw them. In his haste he somehow managed to slip on the glossy surface of the parquet floor, his feet shot out from under, and he came crashing down, hitting his head on the corner of a table. Hours later he was dead.

In the turmoil following the accident the two small packages had been mislaid, and it was only two weeks later, just before the service, that the blue boxes from Tiffany were opened. The girls, who had been traumatized into an almost uncanny stoicism, suddenly broke down when they saw the necklace of cultured pearls for Fredrika and small gold and pearl bracelet for her sister. How ironic that Alfred's lovingly chosen presents would be debuted at his own memorial?

Cruelly, at the reception in the house following the service, many guests exchanged stories about Alfred's fabled awkwardness and bad luck. "Hand him a hammer and he'd smash his thumb" or "Remember the day when he tried to fix his car and it rolled back on him and wrecked his foot? Kept him out of the service, too." Another recalled how, on his honeymoon, Alfred hiccupped for three days, non-stop.

The girls looked on with shock as they saw people, most of them men, laughing and joking together. Is this the way to behave when your good friend's dead? They clung together, hoping that their beloved Aunt Gretchen would leave the kitchen to comfort them. Heart-broken and grim-faced, she had thinned down in the weeks following Alfred's death, but preparing for the large reception had given her a strange *élan*. In the first days after the accident she had been glad to receive the many food offerings from the women of her church, and when it came to planning the menu for the feast at the big event, she turned down a caterer's offer. This was her finest hour. She ruled like a dictator in her kitchen, tyrannizing the crew of Lutheran ladies who attempted to help her.

"Place the hams and the turkeys where the guests can get at them. Careful with that pan of scalloped potatoes. Don't fill the salad bowls too full. Hold off on the pies and cakes until the end," she snapped at them as they ran back and forth from the kitchen.

Two long tables for the food and drinks and a number of uncomfortable little folding chairs had been rented from the funeral parlor. Most of the guests ignored the chairs and stood around in small groups, awkwardly balancing their plates and glasses as they chatted. The teenage friends of the girls gathered around the food, filling their mouths, as if to avoid saying the wrong words.

Once in a while Gretchen would join the guests, her arms around both girls. She did not linger long and suspected rightly that her name was often mentioned in the chitchat around the room. Naturally, there was much talk about Alfred's will, which had been recently published in the *Newfield Bee*: daughters Fredrika and Alberta to receive five-hundred-thousand dollars each, plus the house and the remainder of the estate. As the girls were minors, the family lawyer, Donald Bailey, was appointed legal guardian until they came of age. A lifetime trust had been set up for "my good friend, Gretchen Downs, for her devotion in the care of my children and the house." If Gretchen had been younger and slimmer there might have been malicious comment. All agreed that she deserved it. At Gretchen's death the trust would be dissolved, each daughter receiving half of what remained.

Alfred may have been clumsy at most things, but he was graceful at making money. And generous in bestowing it.

The teenaged heiresses wandered about the room, dazed and uncomfortable as neighbors and distant relatives crushed them with hugs and sentimentality. Fredrika, in particular, seemed to shrink from the excessive emotion. Like her father, she was not demonstrative, but could never be termed cold. She had her father's coloring, too. Her blonde sister had an easier way with people. She was smaller, and better coordinated, a top athlete at school. Al was everyone's favorite.

Many years ago, when the children were up in Gretchen's room, nestled in her bed, they had asked to call her "Aunt Gretchen" instead of "Mrs. Downs" as their father had called her. They had real aunts, but they were far away in places with silly names like Oshkosh.

A few of those "real" aunts were present at the reception. Some were annoyed by the girls' lack of interest in them. One of them, Aunt Lucille, had returned to Oshkosh, deeply offended.

"Really, I don't know what to make of those girls. I even offered to have them live with me, even pay for their education. They weren't even grateful." She sniffed. "Said they'd be happy staying home with 'Aunt Gretchen.' Why, that woman was only a housekeeper! But she sure got her hooks on my poor brother. They say she's set for life. 'Aunt Gretchen' indeed!"

When Gretchen would emerge from the kitchen from time to time, the girls would run to her for refuge, clinging to her, in tears.

"Well, I'm glad to see some emotion," Cousin Lillian said, as she helped herself to another slice of Gretchen's lemon chiffon pie.

Gretchen comforted them. "Go ahead and cry, darlings. This will be the hardest day of your lives, but in a few hours, when all the food and drink is gone, they'll go away, and we'll go up to my room and take care of each other."

2

Jealousy

Ten years had passed since their father's death. The Eliot girls had changed from teenagers into poised young women. Fredrika had grown even taller and had lost much of the awkwardness of her youth. Her posture had improved, and though she no longer slouched to hide her full figure, never would she be mistaken for a model.

Her sister, now known to all as "Al," remained petite, but her personality had greatly expanded. She and her sister had the same wavy hair and small nose of their mother, but Al had a sensual quality that was magnetic. Without question, the local boys rated her a ten. In college she had been a cheerleader and one of the most popular girls on the campus.

Strangely enough, Freddie did not appear jealous of her sister. Half jokingly, she told a friend, "I'm smarter than she is." Actually, she secretly scorned Al's bubbly enthusiasm, and feared that her sister's naïveté might get her into trouble. Freddie was intelligent enough to be aware that her money raised her to a higher level of notice among men. Consequently, she was wary of the local bachelors in the town. Once in a while after receiving special attention from one of them, she would study herself in a full-length mirror. She was not a beauty, she decided, "but not bad, really." Taking an inventory of her assets, she rated her complexion "good, but slightly freckled," eyes and hair above average (though her brows were too thick, like her father's), legs long and well shaped. She rated herself a seven-plus.

Matthew Swenson, who dated her from time to time, would have scored her an eight. He was a thirty-year-old blond bachelor, tall enough at six-three not to be intimated by her height and as the only son of a successful furniture manufacturer, he was not impressed by the Eliot girls' reputed wealth.

One Saturday afternoon in late October, when he was at loose ends, he called Fredrika. As an old friend, he knew that she was not the touchy type and wouldn't be offended by a last-minute invitation.

"Freddie, this is Matt. I don't know 'bout you, but I'm sitting here, bored out of my skull, and I wondered how you'd feel about dinner and a movie tonight. You're probably all signed up for the evening, but I just took a chance that you might be free."

"Free as a bird!" she laughed. And lonely, too, as Gretchen was away for two days visiting a cousin. She was not used to being alone, and the big empty rooms of the old house depressed her. Matt was not the most exciting man in town – not bad looking, a bit heavy, and showing signs of balding – but this was no time to be fussy, she thought as she put down the phone.

What should she wear? she mused. The new silk print? No, that would make her look too needy, too grateful for a date. Perhaps the old navy blue dress would be more suitable, she thought as she laid it on her bed. It had been expensive, but it had served her well for three years. She had always had a good time in it. Matt was not the kind to notice what she wore. One didn't dress for men's opinions anyway. It was the approval of her friends that counted, though she knew that most of them had given up after years of trying to make her stylish.

The doorbell rang as she was making a final check in the mirror. A hot shower had given a becoming flush to her face, and her hair looked better than usual. The old dress still clung in the right places. Not bad for such short notice, she thought, as she smoothed her hair with both hands.

Evidently Matt had also given some thought to his appearance. His glen plaid sports jacket was freshly pressed and his white Brooks Brothers button-down shirt and conservative tie made him look "Ivy League," which he was not.

"The place looks great," he said as he entered the former front parlor. "It now looks like a living room, not a dying room." It was he and a decorator who had transformed the dreary Victorian room into a cheerful, welcoming place.

Freddie was not ready to give him all the credit for the changes. "I don't know if it was too smart getting rid of the old Victorian pieces. They say that stuff is going to get more and more valuable"

"Who is *they?*" he retorted. "What do *they* know? Admit it, that furniture was ugly, uncomfortable and musty smelling. Who needs that?"

His words hurt her, but she tried not to show it. "Well, you did give us a wonderful price on the furniture from your place. Maybe that makes up for the beating we took on the old pieces."

Matt went up to Freddie and gave her a hug. "Darn it, Freddie, you have memory like an elephant. You have a beautiful new room now. Enjoy it!"

For most of its existence the front room of the Eliot house had served as a virtual undertaker's annex, its ancient doors wide enough for a coffin to pass through. In fact, generations of Eliot coffins had been carried through and laid on trestles in the center of the big room, there to be admired or wept over. Alfred's cremation had changed all of that, and Gretchen's memorial feast was spread out where the "remains" had once been displayed.

Since that day the sepulchral look of the place had been completely transformed. The dreary, cigar-smoke-stained wallpaper had been stripped and the walls painted a soft rose. White, delicately embroidered curtains took the place of the heavy, mustard-colored draperies. In carefully planned conversational sections various sofas and easy chairs were placed around the high-ceilinged room. A very large sectional couch and a pair of wing chairs were the room's focus in front of the massive fireplace.

The only remnant of cigar's glory days, when the Eliots made a handsome living farming long-leafed tobacco, was a highly polished antique brass spittoon. Placed in the center of the bay window, it now served as a container for a spectacular fern. Alberta had planted it as a tiny shoot years ago, and it had grown to astonishing size, its greenery lending an exotic atmosphere to the room.

"My God, that thing will bust through the ceiling if you don't watch it. What made it so gigantic? Remnants of all that ancient spittle?" said Matt, laughing.

As usual, Freddie was entertained by Matt's sense of humor. She had known him for years and had always felt a sisterly affection for him. Once or twice he had tried a tentative pass at her, but she felt safe with Matt, and was looking forward to a pleasant, uncomplicated evening with him.

Still admiring the plant, Matt added, "Perhaps you should place a rattan chair under it, give the room a really tropical air. You say your sister planted it? How amazing! By the way, I haven't heard you mention her in some time. Is she still in Ohio?"

"As far as I know," she answered coldly.

Matt immediately regretted that he had brought up the subject. Five years ago Alberta had eloped with George Waters, a handsome young man who had been a beau of her sister. At the time Freddie had tried to hide her humiliation and her fury at her sister, as the whole town had noticed her infatuation with George. From the day she met him she adored him. There was a shyness about him, an appealing diffidence, which reminded her of her father. He was kind and considerate and had blue eyes to die for. Freddie was so bedazzled that she all but stalked him as he walked about town. She dreamed obsessively about him, secretly bought bridal magazines, and was determined to marry him.

George was no fool, and was quite aware of the effect he was having on her, but simply laughed when friends warned him, "Watch out for Freddie Eliot. She's gone bananas over you, and she's a girl who usually gets what she wants."

Being of a warm and affectionate nature, he did nothing to cool her ardor. Her caresses and eager kisses were returned, though Freddie failed to notice that his were more polite than romantic. George was not unkind and did not mean to encourage the young woman, but as everyone said, "He's a nice guy, but not too bright."

Unfortunately for Freddie, who had been living in a dream of matrimonial joy, Alberta appeared on the scene. She had been traveling for several months. When she and George met, poor Freddie's chances were shipwrecked. The electricity between George and Alberta crackled with such fire that people who watched them together felt like voyeurs at an erotic film. Their subsequent elopement to Ohio, a few weeks later, did not surprise anyone, not even Freddie. She had been beaten by a primal force and knew it. Humiliation made her leave town for a while as she visited a college friend in Florida.

On her return people tried to act naturally with her, but it was obvious that they were running out of tact. Only Matt had the courage to say what others were thinking: "What a lousy trick to pull on your own sister."

To his surprise, she replied defensively, "She couldn't help herself. I can't blame her – or him, for that matter."

"You're amazing! You really believe that, don't you?"

"Yes, Matt, I really do. But I doubt if I'll ever see or hear from them again." With that, she buried her head on Matt's shoulder and cried her eyes out.

He had been a staunch friend to her from that time and over the years they had enjoyed each other's company, though no man had since excited her in the way that George had.

She did make an effort to see others, and Gretchen constantly nagged her, "Give some little dinner parties. Invite a few congenial friends. I'd love to cook you a special meal."

She had found that entertaining was easier at home than going out. Every time she was seen in a restaurant with a new man the local gossip would start, as he would be carefully assessed and ultimately rated as inappropriate as a suitor of Fredrika Eliot, the town's most eligible single woman. Simon Hart, a longhaired writer; Norm Peters, a baby-faced banker; and Gerald Blakemore, a slightly effeminate interior designer – all failed their tests. Matthew Swenson might have received an endorsement, but he was old news.

His call and last minute invitation had come at a critical time for Freddie, the fifth anniversary of Al and George's runaway to Ohio. The date had been stamped on her memory: October 19, 1973. Al had been only 20 then, Freddie mused. Too young to have known what she was doing. Perhaps it was time to forgive and forget. At least to *forget*. Five years of hatred, she told herself, was five years too long. Suddenly she felt a sense of release, as if a large rock had been lifted off her back. It was time to shed all the anger that had been eroding her for so long.

A lightness had come over her as she thought of her date with Matt and set two glasses and a bottle of Jack Daniel's, Matt's favorite, on the coffee table. She was determined to have a good time.

"No coke for you?" he asked as he sat down on the couch. For the past five years Freddie had not smoked or taken a drink.

She smiled. "I think it's about time for me to step out into the world again. Let's relax, and have a good time tonight."

A good time? What could that mean? He glanced at his old friend. She was looking a bit different, had a special glow that he hadn't seen in years. Had she finally shaken off the insecurities that had plagued her for so long? There was a new confidence about her. She looked different. She smelled different. Was she using a new scent, or was it simply his imagination, he wondered, as he made himself a drink.

Freddie shuddered at first as she began to sip her whiskey. Then she took a swallow, and then another. This was pleasant. It had been years since she had felt that kind of warmth seeping through her body.

"Sorry I don't have even a potato chip to go with this."

"Forget it. I've made a dinner reservation for seven-thirty. The movie goes on at nine fifteen." He checked his watch. "I guess we'd better shove off."

3

Regret

Caruso's was not a particularly attractive restaurant, nor was it noted for its food, but for some mysterious reason it was the most popular place in Newfield, a town whose population now passed 20,000. With its standard red-checked tablecloths and well-worn burgundy leather booths, it had a lived-in look. Even its waiters – most of them veterans of many years – had that look. People felt comfortable there, generations of them. An upscale French place had had but a short life in Newfield. All that *nouvelle cuisine* didn't sit well with a farm community. That restaurant had moved to Hartford, where it flourished.

As usual, Caruso's had its regular Saturday night crowd – young and old couples, singles packed around the bar, and in a back room, two or three family groups were noisily celebrating a birthday or wedding anniversary.

At Caruso's Matt never had to look at a menu. "That'll be a Jack Daniel's, a side of spaghetti and the veal *Marsala* for you. And what for the lady?" the waiter asked. He looked over at Freddie. She seemed more relaxed than usual, less stiff, he thought. Freddie was not one of his favorites.

She was slow to answer. Already she was starting to feel somewhat light-headed. "That drink at my place was pretty strong. I guess I was out of practice. Maybe a glass of white wine? You choose. The veal sounds perfect, but no spaghetti. Meanwhile, I think I'd better zip off to the powder room." She hurried out, pushing her way through the crowd.

Her face felt flushed and she needed to splash some water on it. It was ridiculous to feel this way, she told herself, after only one drink. Or was it only one? As she returned to the table she tried to remember. She picked up her glass, which was of generous size, and filled to the top. After two long swallows she felt more in control.

"What am I drinking? It tastes really good. You say it's Chablis?"

She did not object when the waiter deftly refilled her glass a few minutes later. The wine had made her calmer, less intense. Matt, too, seemed to be acting more relaxed as they slowly enjoyed their dinner.

He leaned closer to her across the table.

"Freddie and Al. I've always wondered how you two got such boyish names. Isn't that what they called you at school, 'The Boys'?"

She made a grimace before answering. "I've gotten used to it now, but it wasn't easy. Dad was dead set on having a son named Alfred. And our names, Alberta and Fredrika, were as close as he could get. Pretty tacky, I guess, but I'm stuck with it."

"Yet he never tried to bring you up as boys," he laughed. "You and Al are definitely feminine. No question about that, and very attractive, too, honey." He moved his face closer to hers.

Quickly, she picked up the desert menu and hid behind it. "Do we have time for something before the movie?" she asked.

It had been years since she had heard her sister discussed. *Feminine* surely described Al, she thought. The woman exuded waves of sensuality whenever she walked into a room. It was a relief to her when the subject was changed as Matt paid the bill and they set off for the movie house.

She had hoped to see *Saturday Night Fever*, an R-rated film, which had played to record crowds. It would mean a long drive to Hartford, so both decided to see the old Charles Boyer and Ingrid Bergman murder mystery, *Gaslight*, which was the latest in the series of movie classics that the local theater showed once a month. The feature had already started by the time they arrived, so they had to grope around in the dark before they found two seats off to one side. Freddie kept on her lightweight coat. Past experience with certain men had proved that it was a wise move, and Matt, for some reason, had seemed less brotherly than usual. Or had she imagined it? The unaccustomed drinks had made her feel uncertain, but she was still sober enough to be wary. She felt more secure inside her coat, and she did not move away when Matt put an arm around her shoulder.

Charles Boyer had always been her favorite actor. With his velvet eyes and sultry French accent alone, he could heat up the screen. In Boyer movies there was no heavy breathing, no writhing bodies. Those eyes and that voice did it all. She particularly remembered one seduction scene some years ago, when his hands had glided down the silken back of a woman's dress, and slowly, oh so slowly, pulled down the zipper, all the while caressing her with his voice. Fade out. One's imagination filled in the rest.

But, with *Gaslight*, it was the plot – with its intricate and carefully woven psychological aspects – that attracted her attention even more than Boyer's looks and smooth manner. She thought the murderer had indeed crafted the perfect crime. But even Charles Boyer couldn't get away with murder!

As they walked, arm in arm, out of the theater Matt said, "I never could see why so many women went gaga over Boyer. To me, he's too soft. Look at those eyes, and those lashes. Almost feminine. Now take Gable. There's a real man."

"Yes, I'll take *him* too," laughed Freddie as Matt helped her into his car. "There's not much suspense with Gable, though. He's all action. His eyes twinkle, they don't smolder."

"What about *your* eyes? Would you call them twinklers or smolderers?" Matt asked as he took her face between his hands.

She was starting to feel a bit uncomfortable.

"Let's settle for friendly."

Matt paused before starting the motor. "What do you say we go to Rafters for a while, dance a little, and have some drinks?"

"Drinks? I don't know . . . but I haven't danced for ages. It might be fun."

"It's always fun at Rafters. Never been to Rafters? I'm surprised," he said, though he wasn't surprised at all.

In high school Freddie used to hear about Rafters. It was not a place for nice girls, Gretchen had told her. The "fast crowd" went there to drink, dance and "behave like sluts." Well, Gretchen was away for a few days, she mused, so she needn't worry about confronting her.

"I'm a big girl now, and I think it's about time for me to go to Rafters. Part of my education," she laughed. Suddenly she felt more relaxed.

Neither spoke much on the six-mile drive. When they arrived at Rafters there was the usual Saturday night jam in the parking lot, but Matt managed to shoehorn his car into a space. As she watched his skillful maneuvers Freddie recalled her father's frustrations at the wheel.

"My dad would have taken all night to squeeze into that spot."

"Let's face it, Honey, your father was a sweetheart, but coordination wasn't his thing," said Matt. "But he was pretty skillful in other ways." As he spoke he was thinking that Alfred Eliot may have seemed clumsy and naïve, but nobody could beat him when it came to making money. He wondered if either of the Eliot girls had any idea how rich they were.

Freddie did not have her sister's looks and sex appeal, but she was certainly attractive. Strange that she had never married. Tonight, he thought, she looked more interesting than usual. He noticed a new relaxation, a new aura about her. Could it be the drinks that had removed some of the tension and reserve of her personality, made her seem more approachable? Perhaps Rafter's atmosphere would unleash some of her hang-ups. He'd seen it work with other girls.

"Well, what do you think?" he asked as he led her to a table. "Looks like an old English tavern, with those dark timbers, doesn't it?"

Hardly, she thought. The pseudo-Tudor décor did not impress her. The place was far too crowded and smoky, but everybody seemed to be having a good time, and she determined to enjoy herself.

"Want to sample a different drink?" he said as he ordered two Planter's Punches. "It was popular a few years ago, but as a summer drink. It's mostly rum and fruit juice. I think you'll like it."

He watched her as she took her first sip from a straw. "Goes down easy, doesn't it?"

Indeed it does, she thought, as she finished one tall glass and started a second. Between drinks they danced. Freddie was happy to feel less clumsy than usual, and avoided stepping on Matt's feet. A sense of euphoria was creeping over her, a glow that made the room seem more attractive, less smoky. The dancers around her smiled at her more often, made her feel more welcome in their company. Some inner glow gave her the confidence to step out on the dance floor alone, her third Planter's Punch in one hand. She was very, very drunk – and didn't know it.

When she woke up two hours later she was lying on a bed in a small, musty room, with no memory of having stumbled up the stairs. The room was cast in semi-darkness. She was not alone. As her head cleared and her eyes began to focus, she noticed a figure on the bed beside her. It was Matt, and he was snoring. She dimly remembered his last words to her, "Drink up, girl, it's good for you."

Gradually her vision improved and she noticed that she was lying *on* the bed, not in it. She also saw that her new red pumps were lying on the floor, her stockings lay a few feet away. My God! What had she done! At 28, Fredrika Eliot was still a virgin, or so she hoped. Her upper body felt sore, her lips were swollen and there was a rip at the neck of her dress. Her legs and lower thighs were exposed. The skirt of her dress had been bunched around her waist. Gingerly, she ran her hands down the rest of her body and suddenly felt her panty girdle. Praise be, it was still intact! Never had she felt such a relief. A friend had once referred to her panty girdle as "my chastity belt!"

She looked over at Matt curled in a fetal position beside her. His shoes and trousers had been tossed on the floor. From the waist up he was totally dressed – the Glen plaid jacket, button-down shirt, even his tie, were in place. In any other situation she would have burst out laughing as she saw his boxer shorts. They were of white silk, patterned with red and green circles that read "Stop!" and "Go!"

Even though it seemed as if "nothing had happened," she hurried to leave the room before Matt woke up. At a small basin and mirror in the back of the room she washed her face and hands and ran her pocket comb through her hair before tiptoeing down the stairs, her pumps in her hands.

Tom Langan, owner of Rafters, was busy cleaning up the bar when he saw the puffy-eyed, disheveled young woman approaching him. He often witnessed such scenes, but this woman looked more mature than his usual customers. There was a weariness about her, or was it shock, as she weaved towards him, carrying a pair of shoes.

Whatever happened up there, it wasn't fun, he thought, as he saw the tear in her dress. "Are you O.K., Miss?" he asked as he continued wiping a cloth over the bar top. Keep calm, he told himself.

"Not exactly. I have to find some way to get home." She tried hard to keep her voice from shaking as she sat on a chair and with trembling hands, attempted to slip on her pumps.

"Here, let me help you." He knelt down. "Do you need a doctor?" (Please, God, don't get the police into this.) "You look pretty bad. What went on up there?"

None of your damned business, she thought. "No, I don't need a doctor, just someone to drive me to Newfield. It's about six miles."

"I can find you a driver, but at this hour it'll cost some bucks."

She thankfully remembered the "mad money" that Gretchen had always urged her to carry. "Would twenty dollars be enough?"

Easy money for his pal, Jake, who had helped in such situations before. "My friend John Burns runs a taxi service. He can be over in five minutes. He looked sharply at her. "You look as if you could use a drink."

"Heavens, no! But thanks."

They waited in silence until they heard the sound of the taxi. Tom helped her into the car. What a relief to have her leave his place. He listened as Freddie told the driver, "Eliot Farm. It's about six miles away, just outside of Newfield."

She sat in the backseat, glad to be alone in the darkness of the cab. The two of them kept a tactful silence as they traveled east through backcountry roads. It was almost five-thirty. The light was beginning to change from gray to rose as the rising sun could be glimpsed through the tall pines. Freddie closed her eyes and tried to shut out both past and present.

To Burns at the wheel, the words "Eliot Farm" had a familiar sound. The Eliots, he recalled, were once rich tobacco growers in the Connecticut Valley. Maybe this strange woman in the back seat was an Eliot. Maybe she could pay a lot more than twenty bucks for the short ride home. Maybe he should take the longer route?

Suddenly from behind him, he heard from his passenger, a sort of choking sound. Was she sobbing, or was she laughing? Better not ask. He'd seen women in this condition before. Better take the short way. He tried to hear what she was saying. Something about a panty girdle?

Hysterical women were not his favorite passengers. He drove as fast as he could, took the twenty dollars, and supported her as she shakily climbed the porch steps.

✶ ✶ ✶ ✶ ✶ ✶

Hours later, Matt woke up as the sun was beginning to filter through the shuttered windows. He was alone in the dingy, narrow room. It was very quiet, save for the chirping of birds as they stirred in the tree outside. There was no sign of Freddie, only the mark of her body on the bedspread. My God! What had happened, he thought as he painfully raised himself to a sitting position on the bed. Planter's Punch indeed. That drink packed a wallop, not a punch. The sight of his bare thighs in their ridiculous shorts gave him a shock. Obviously he must have tried something with his old friend Freddie, the girl who had always been like a sister to him. The untouchable. What an idiot he had been to put her in such a situation. Cruel, too.

It did not take long for him to pull on his trousers, slap some water on his face and walk downstairs to pay his bill. As he thought about Freddie a cold sweat came over him. He felt nauseated, and his head pounded. He had done a lot of stupid things in his life, but this one topped them all.

"Your girl friend sneaked out on you? She looked a mess. What the Hell were you doing up there?" asked the owner sardonically. "Lucky for you she didn't call the police."

Matt was too shaken to reply.

"And lucky I got Jake to drive her home," Tom Langan continued. "In the future find another place to take your dates. I don't need your kind of trouble," he snarled.

On his arrival home he went straight to bed. Later he called his office and reported sick. For three days he was afraid to go out, fearful of running into Freddie. Finally he took a deep breath and dialed her number.

"Freddie, this is Matt."

"Yes, I recognized the voice." Her tone was even chillier than he had expected.

"About the other night what can I say?"

"Don't even try." There was a click and the phone went dead.

Matt felt as if he had been kicked in the stomach, and he knew he deserved it. It would be years before he and Freddie became friends again.

4

Rebound

Gretchen never knew of Freddie's fiasco with Matt. From time to time she would ask, "What ever became of your friend Matthew Swenson? Don't you like him any more? Did something happen between you two?" Gretchen tried to avoid being nosy, but Matt was her favorite among Freddie's men.

"Nothing happened." Freddie replied crossly. Nothing at all, thank God. The humiliation on both sides had been beyond repair. In a small town it was impossible to escape occasional meetings. At parties they were polite to each other, made the usual small talk, then fled to opposite ends of the room. If anyone noticed the chill between them there were no comments. Only Gretchen remained concerned.

Occasionally Freddie dated other men. They found her company amusing, but rather a disappointment when they attempted more intimacy. Some, like Matt, had tried to talk her into taking a drink, but soon discovered their mistake.

"No, thanks. I get silly enough without alcohol," she'd protest. "Just be happy that I'm such a cheap date."

And they were, for the most part. But two men, David Black and Gus Johnson, wanted more than she was ready to give. After some frustrating encounters they both left in search of more cooperative women.

"Darling, forget them. They weren't your sort," Gretchen would console her.

"Just what is my 'sort'?" Freddie would respond. She often wondered herself just what she would call herself – a snob, an icy bitch, a woman wary of being wooed for her money?

"When the right man comes along, you'll know it."

How tired she was of hearing those words. Well, the "right man" had come along, many years ago, and was now living in Ohio with Al. It had been a long time since she had thought of her sister. Did she still have that magic, the allure to attract every man in the room? Was it an inborn talent, or did one have to work at it?

Freddie was too much of a realist to attempt to glamorize herself. Makeup can do just so much. It's the inner self that must be developed. She had once read in a woman's magazine that "to be interesting to men you must expand your interests. Become a sports enthusiast, a skier, for instance. That's where the men are, and even if you're a real clod on the slopes, those beautiful ski clothes can do wonders for you *après ski.*"

Accordingly, she went to New York where she set about to buy the most expensive ski outfits she could find: the skis, boots, and finally the most colorful, chic clothes. It would have been smart to have a ski-wise friend accompany her, but she felt a bit shy about telling anyone of her search for the "right" man.

In retrospect, the idea had been a good one, she mused. Unfortunately, like her father, she had been unlucky. On her very first day, even before she had put on her ski boots, she slipped on the ice at the entrance to the lodge and broke her leg in two places. So much for "finding your man on the slopes."

While recuperating at home, after a stay in the hospital, Freddie browsed through a catalog from a community college in Hartford. Two courses had special appeal: *Creative Writing*, and *Art for Beginners*. Perhaps the course on investing, "*How to make your money work for you*," would have been a better way to meet new men, but art and writing had always interested her.

At any rate she had more or less given up the search for "Mr. Right." Her last attempt, a two-week cruise on a riverboat in France, was a flop. The ship was comfortable. She had booked a single cabin on the top deck and enjoyed the views of the Rhone River towns as they glided by, but socially it was a disaster. Her fellow passengers were pleasant and tried to include her in their conversations. They were middle- aged retired persons, most of them married, and she had nothing in common with them. As an attractive, single woman she may have presented a threat to some of the wives on board. There were four single men among the forty passengers: two of them were witty and intelligent, but completely absorbed in themselves, much like a honeymoon couple; the others were either too fat or too old.

Obviously, she had to find another way to enrich her life, which, as she was aware, had become stale. None of the courses in the catalog sounded very exciting, but who knows, they might put a little spark into her routine. In her mind, she was a thirty-year-old nobody, going nowhere.

The writing course attracted her, as she had once toyed with the idea of writing a cooking column for the local paper. As a volunteer at her church she had written a small, spiral-bound cookbook, which had been sold for charity. It was not an ordinary cookbook, chock full of recipes, but a sort of witty diary of her triumphs and failures as a cook. She even had the temerity to illustrate it with some stick figures of herself at work. It was very amateurish, but she was proud of it, and it had raised quite a bit of money for the missionary work of the church.

It was a small writing class, made up of disappointed women, like her, who were looking for a new direction in their growth. There was not much joy in their lives, it would seem, and it showed in their work. Dreary after dreary story was read aloud each week. After six weeks Freddie left the class, too depressed to continue.

The art class was another story. It was a larger, happier group. Freddie found a number of talented and carefree souls with whom she quickly made friends. One of them was Patrick Nelson. He was two or three inches taller than she, of strong build, and his mass of dark curls made him a standout among the other three men in the class. Patrick and Freddie enjoyed each other's company, laughed at the same jokes. Sometimes after class they would meet – "Dutch treat" – in the nearby coffee shop.

"I'm at that dangerous stage," he once told her. "The post-divorce time, when I'm particularly susceptible. Consider yourself warned." He reached across the table and took her hand. She did not draw away. He was extremely attractive, yet, at the same time she was wary. Who was this man?

"What do you do in 'civilian' life?" she asked him with a smile.

Nothing interesting, he told her. Like many young men in the Hartford area, he was in the insurance business. "Up to now insurance has been my life and my meal ticket, too. Right now I'm at the crossroads, wondering which turn in the road to take. I'd always wanted to be a graphic artist. Don't ask me why. So I'm learning art at the basic level. What about you?"

What could she tell him? That she was a lonely, bored thirty-year-old single woman of independent means and minor standing in a small town on the fringe of Hartford. Should she tell him that the real romance of her life had ended in disaster, and sent her into a deep freeze forever? No, tell him nothing. If he was really interested, he'll find out, more than he might want to know, she mused. Perhaps he might like to know that I'm a damned good cook.

5

Entertaining

Ever since she was a child Freddie had watched Gretchen in the kitchen, and learned bit by bit, how to measure, how to stir, how to use a whisk, a spatula, or a boning knife. Timing, one of the most important elements in successful baking, took longer to master, but she eventually learned by instinct just when her cakes and pies had reached perfection: not overcooked and dry, or undercooked and wet inside. Even Gretchen was surprised at Freddie's growing expertise. On Fridays, Gretchen's day off, Freddie loved to entertain a few friends (rarely more than six at a time) and tried out new recipes.

Her new friend, Patrick, had not been too impressed with her artwork, but perhaps if he could taste one of her specialties, *seafood crêpe* or *lemon chiffon pie*, he might appreciate her talent as a cook. On the other hand, it might be unwise to make the first move. She must plan her strategy with care.

"Tell me, honestly, do you think I'm wasting my time on this art class?" she asked one evening. "It's been three months now, and I can see that *you've* improved, but my drawing has hardly progressed beyond the kindergarten level. I'm not fishing for kudos. Just tell me the truth."

"Sure you want to know?" he asked, smiling.

"I think I already know your answer. 'Stick with the writing course.' Well, I dropped out of that some weeks ago."

"What happened?"

"I just couldn't take any more sordid stories about wife beating, child abuse and desperate poverty. What twisted minds those women have!"

They both laughed as she continued, "I do have some skill in a different direction. Come to my house and I'll cook you a meal that will make your stomach cry for more."

There, she'd done it, made the first move.

✶ ✶ ✶ ✶ ✶ ✶

Patrick was rather surprised when he arrived at the Eliot Farm the following Friday evening. He knew that Freddie had some money, but was not prepared for the dignity and elegance of the high roofed Victorian house. With its intricate, gingerbread ornamentation, the place had long been an architectural landmark in the area. The designer had controlled his urge to add a fashionable tower to an already tall house, and had kept assorted projections to a minimum. The result was a pleasing, well balanced, welcoming home. One of its most attractive features was the extra-wide porch, or veranda, which wrapped around the front and one side of the house.

As he parked his car on the circular, graveled driveway, he saw no other cars, and wondered if he were the only guest. He walked six steps to the front door, which was opened by Freddie. Over a formal, long black skirt she was wearing a no-nonsense white apron.

She laughed as she saw the look on his face. "Most people are surprised when they first come here. It isn't exactly a Charles Adams kind of place, with all kinds of spooky little nooks and crannies, but it was fashionable when the Eliots had it built in 1868, in the boom times after the Civil War. All those little gimcracks went out of style years ago, but I love it." She'd planned originally to invite some others, she said, "But frankly, I'm looking forward to showing off my cooking just for you. You see, I have to prove myself."

He noticed her flushed cheeks. Was it an unusual elation in her personality that he had not seen before, or was it simply the heat from her kitchen?

She led him past the impressive, high-ceilinged living room and into the smaller, cozier den, where a dining table had been set for two. It was too warm for a fire in the Franklin stove, so she had banked it with fresh flowers, a trick she had seen in a magazine. She had never fussed this way before, nor found herself so keyed up. Not since the days of George had she been so excited about a man.

"Please make yourself a drink," she said as she showed him a small bar in a corner of the room. "I'm having a ginger ale myself, but don't let that stop you. Years ago I found that alcohol and I don't get along."

As if reading his mind, she added with a laugh, "No I'm not a reformed drunk, nothing that exciting."

Sipping his second Scotch and water, Patrick nibbled on another shrimp. She put a platter of devilled eggs before him. "No fancy *hors d'oeuvres*, I'm afraid. The good stuff will come later."

✶ ✶ ✶ ✶ ✶ ✶

She was indeed right, thought Patrick. "The other day you asked me if you were wasting your time in that art course. Well, the answer is an emphatic yes. Lady, you're a born chef. Can't remember when I've had a more delectable dinner. The filet mignon was incredible, and that dessert was a winner. Seriously, have you ever contemplated starting a restaurant?"

Blushing with pleasure, she answered. "Some friends have suggested it, but the restaurant game is so damned risky."

"And you're not risky? Is that why you're still *Miss* Fredrika Eliot of Eliot Farm?"

Oops, he'd said too much.

"And why *your* risk didn't take," she said, smiling.

"Touché! I had no right to ask that question."

There was a silence, and then rather hesitantly she confessed, "There was a time when I was a risk taker. Many years ago, when I was twenty, I met a man I was crazy about. Fell ass over teakettle as the old saying goes. I was so far gone I'd have taken any risk to marry him. Made a total fool out of myself."

"And then?"

"And then my sexy little sister, Alberta, spotted him and ate him alive."

On impulse, Patrick reached out and put his arms around her. She began to sob and could not stop, her face on his shoulder. Finally, in a shaky voice, she said, "There, I've done it again – made another fool of myself."

Quickly she set about cleaning off the table. This was not the evening she had planned. Plaudits she wanted, not pity.

6

Decline

"How did your dinner go off?" Gretchen asked the following day.

"He didn't stay long," came the reply.

Guess the evening wasn't a success, thought Gretchen. How sad. The poor girl had been all wound up, really excited about planning a meal for this new man.

For more than twenty years Gretchen had been emotionally caught in the web of the Eliot girls' lives. In troubled times she worried about them and in happy times she rejoiced with them. Ten years ago Alberta had gone off, Lord knows where, and Gretchen rarely thought of her. Fredrika's future was another matter. She continued to wonder what had caused the break between her and Matthew Swenson? Of all the men she'd seen around the house, he was her favorite.

In 1980 women seemed to be marrying later, Gretchen mused, as "women's lib" had opened more careers for them, but Fredrika stayed home, seemingly content. Of course she did not need the money, was not Hell-bent on proving something. Careers were all very well for women who wanted to get out of the house, but Fredrika loved her house, was at her happiest when she and Gretchen were cooking together.

It was rather a relief, Gretchen thought, for Fredrika to take on more of the cooking and some of the household chores, though a part-time cleaning woman now helped to keep the house in order. Arthritis was beginning to insinuate itself into parts of her body. It started with her hands, then her wrists and worked its way down her spine, but she did not complain. She was determined to avoid being a tiresome whiner, like some of her friends. Slowing down was not natural to her, but when pains began in her stomach she started to worry. All her life she had been robust and vigorous, twice as active as women half her age, but now she had to sit down more frequently, rest, and cut down on desserts. She had never worried about her health before, but memories of her mother's agonizing death from cancer when she was only 60 began to obsess her.

Freddie tried to hide her anxiety about her beloved Aunt Gretchen. There was something terribly wrong going on in that elderly body, she knew. The clothes hung loosely on her as she walked with ever slowing steps through the house, and climbing the stairs to her third-floor room had become more and more difficult.

Both of them continued pretending to each other that all was well. One day Freddie stopped playing the game.

"Dear Aunt Gretchen," she said, "Wouldn't it make sense for you to move downstairs? That climb must be killing you."

The word "killing" was unfortunate. Gretchen went into a rare fit of temper. "Leave my room! What a crazy idea. I may be slowing up, but there's plenty of life in me yet."

And that was that.

Freddie's attempts to persuade Gretchen to see a doctor were equally rebuffed.

"No, no, darling. You fuss too much. I may have lost a little weight, but that's not bad. I always was kinda heavy. I don't need a doctor. Don't want him to go poking around in my insides. I'm just a little tired, that's all."

For once in her busy life, however, Gretchen finally agreed to take an afternoon nap in the den, but not until – with much effort – she had tidied up her kitchen. Every once in a while Freddie would peer in to check on her. One day, when she saw Gretchen looking even more pale and frail than usual, she finally called the doctor.

Evan Blackford and his father before him had been taking care of the Eliots for three generations. He rarely made house calls, but when he got the word about Gretchen, who was, after all, part of the Eliot family, he responded quickly. He was led into the den where she was lying on the couch, her favorite afghan tucked around her. She frowned when she saw the doctor.

She scolded him as he hurried toward her, medicine kit in hand. "Doctor, Fredrika disobeyed me. She shouldn't have called you. Imagine making house calls these days. At your age, you shouldn't be working so hard."

"Look who's talking," he teased. "I'll bet you're no younger than I am."

Gretchen was touchy about revealing her age. "That's my business." Her voice had lost most of its snap. She attempted to look cross, but the doctor could tell that she was secretly relieved when he took out his stethoscope and began to examine her.

"I'll be in the kitchen if you need me," Freddie told him.

A few minutes later he came into the kitchen. From his expression Freddie could guess that bad news was coming. His diagnosis was no surprise: with his probing fingers he had found a lump in Gretchen's belly. "It doesn't look good, and we'll have to put her in the hospital for further tests. As you and I know, getting her into a hospital is going to be rough, but her chances look poor, and there's no other way to save her."

Freddie had braced herself for a battle with Gretchen about going to the hospital. Strangely enough, her reaction to the doctor's verdict had been much more passive than expected. Within two hours, without protest, she was in an ambulance – with Freddie beside her – on her way to the Hartford Hospital. It was Gretchen's very silence – her compliance – that broke Freddie's heart. The life force, the spirit, seemed to have been plucked out of her. She held Gretchen's hand and tried not to weep.

✷ ✷ ✷ ✷ ✷ ✷

Freddie's days were spent at the hospital in Gretchen's private room. Much of the time Gretchen was dozing, almost in a semi-comatose state. Silently sitting by the edge of the bed, Freddie felt as if she were with a stranger. There was a body there, but it was not Gretchen. Hour after hour, she kept up the vigil, hoping for a miracle. After eight hours of tension, Freddie always felt drained, emotionally and physically, but she still had enough energy to go twice a week to her art class. The very thought of the class gave her a spiritual cocktail, a much needed pick-me-up.

Her drawing skill was as inadequate as ever, but that was unimportant. It was the *après* class time that gave her the lift. At first she had been uncomfortable with Patrick after the emotional ending of their evening at her house, but to Patrick she had become much more interesting. He had since heard of the well-known Eliot girls, learned of the famous nickname, "The Boys." She had only hinted at the problem with her sister. He knew nothing of the scandalous elopement. Whatever had happened, she had been deeply scarred. That might explain some of Freddie's reserve. He was happy to see that beneath her poise and confidence, she was vulnerable.

He noticed her pallor and drooping shoulders as they entered the coffee shop.

"You look wiped out. Is something wrong?"

Once again he saw her starting to break down, mouth trembling, eyes filled with tears.

"It's about Aunt Gretchen. I don't think she's going to make it."

"She's the one who brought you up. The one who still lives with you?" He knew about her devotion to this woman.

Freddie grabbed a paper napkin and dabbed at her eyes as she told him of her mother's death, then of her father's death, and how Gretchen had served as a proxy mother through the years, and how a trust fund had been set up "so she could stay with us and care for us."

Patrick tried to avoid another tearful scene. "And don't forget, she also taught you how to become a wonderful cook."

Her distress could not be diverted. "You'll laugh at this, but the hardest part for me is being alone in that big house. I see her everywhere, can't put her out of my thoughts. I know that pretty soon I'll never see her again, never hear her warning me about men, telling me how to behave like a lady or teaching me how to make the best pecan pie in the world."

She started crying again as Patrick led her to the parking lot. "Would you feel better if I went home with you?" He paused, then added, "And spent the night at your place?"

That was the night when Patrick Nelson and Fredrika Eliot became lovers.

7

Homecoming

Lying with Patrick in her parents' ancient four-poster bed, Freddie felt totally at peace. Though she never had slept with a man before, it seemed to her as if it were the most natural thing in the world. He was loving, he was kind, and above all, he was comforting. For the next ten days they stayed together. Patrick commuted in his car to his job in Hartford while Freddie spent long hours in the hospital. Freddie once wondered, as she looked at Gretchen, what she would have thought had she known that a stranger was sleeping in the Eliots' ancestral bed. Horrified? Or happy to know that someone one was bringing her beloved Fredrika some comfort? It was indeed a comfort to her when she finally arrived home, to find that Patrick had come home earlier, and prepared dinner for them.

"It's not Escoffier, but it's wonderful." She said gratefully. Never had she been so exhausted or happier.

The hospital called at five A.M. to tell her of Gretchen's death. "Very peacefully" they'd said. Was this what was always said, she wondered. It was hard to imagine Gretchen giving up her spirit without a struggle. For a moment, she felt nothing. Then reality hit her, and Patrick tried in vain to ease her anguish. Her sobs eventually subsided as she dressed and went into the kitchen. There was much to do, but first she must make a good, substantial meal for breakfast, Gretchen would have insisted on it.

Upstairs, Patrick was gathering up his things. It was time for him to leave. The house would soon be filled with family and friends of Gretchen and Fredrika. Before he left, she fed him a ham omelet and some English muffins.

"When will I see you again?" he asked as they kissed.

"Darling, I'm too confused right now. I'll be smothered in red tape for a while, but I'll phone you when things are clearer."

News of Gretchen's death traveled with amazing speed. The Lutheran minister, whom Freddie had called to make memorial plans, had already heard the word from the undertaker, who had been called by the hospital to remove the body. And the doctor broke the news to his pal, Donald Bailey, the Eliots' lawyer. Only the *Newfield Bee* failed to get a scoop on the story, so they phoned Freddie for details.

"Her many friends in the Ladies' Guild of the Lutheran Church knew her far longer than I," she said. "I can only tell you that she was a wonderful person, even more than a mother to me."

Predictably, the Guild ladies had been disappointed when they heard that Gretchen would be cremated. This would mean a simpler finale for their old friend, a prime booster in all of their church affairs. But they were not surprised. Had she not said, years ago, at Alfred's memorial reception, "Cremation is a good, sensible thing, but I don't like this idea of scattering ashes all over the place. When I go, just put me in the ground, with a marker over me, so's they'll know I once walked this earth."

As she made the arrangements at the cemetery, Freddie thought to herself how happy Gretchen would be to know that there was room for her urn in the Eliot family plot. The cremation had taken place very quickly, but as in Alfred's case, the church service would be held two weeks later.

"Of course there's a lot of legal tape to plow through," said Donald Bailey. "You and your sister are Gretchen's legal heirs, and as you know, her trust fund reverts to you both. By the way, have you called Alberta about Gretchen's death?"

Freddie answered, bitterly, "You know very well that we haven't spoken in years. Would you mind trying to reach her?"

His attempts to find her had been difficult. For a few years, after her departure from town with George Waters, Bailey had kept in touch with Alberta with Christmas cards, but eventually these had been returned, "address unknown."

"Freddie would be terribly upset if her sister did not return for the memorial ceremony," Bailey told Patrick one day as they lunched together.

Half-jokingly, Patrick suggested, "Perhaps if she knew that Gretchen's trust fund awaited her she might come home in a hurry."

The lawyer was a nice man but never achieved high marks for humor. "With that in mind, our office has been trying to track her down ever since Gretchen's death. It may be weeks before we reach her."

✶ ✶ ✶ ✶ ✶ ✶

On the day of the service many of the Guild members at the Lutheran church competed to take part in furnishing the banquet for the reception.

Never have I seen so many covered dishes," sighed Freddie. "What do they think this is, a pot luck supper?"

In honor of Gretchen, she had hoped to prepare the entire menu, then found too many other duties. The possibility of her sister's impending arrival was troubling enough. "I can't prevent her from coming. This is her house, too, and she loved Gretchen as much as I do, but the very thought of her arriving gives me a knot in my stomach," she said to Patrick.

He laughed a bit stiffly. "I'll be happy to act as a buffer state between the warring sisters," he offered.

"If you really want to be helpful, move your stuff out of my bedroom. It's going to be thorny enough welcoming a long-lost sister without having to ward off malicious gossip, Freddie answered.

"Incidentally, did you plan to introduce me as your fiancé?"

"Don't rush me, darling. Let's play it by ear," she said.

A few days before, Bailey had called to tell her that Alberta had finally been located. She had been hesitant at first about returning, but, as Patrick predicted, the lure of some money drew her home.

They were still talking when they heard the doorbell. "Oh, my God, she's here," Freddie cried as she saw a chunky, gray haired woman standing in the doorway. Surely, thought she, that drab little figure couldn't be the sex goddess who had run off with George Waters, ten years ago. The sisters stared at each other, unsure whether to glare or smile at each other.

Freddie decided to embrace her. "Oh, Al, you made it!" Seconds later she stepped back and looked hard at her sister. "It is Al, isn't it?"

"Yes, dear, it's me, the bad girl come back home. I was so scared, but I just had to come," she said hoarsely.

Looking at the mousy, seedy figure, Patrick thought of course she had to come. She needs the money. He had imagined a blonde siren, a woman of great sexuality, and saw instead an overweight, badly dressed, middle-aged woman. (Actually she was only 27.) He tried to hide his shock as she approached him.

Pathetically attempting an arch look, she said, "And you are Freddie's husband?"

"Well, you could call me her fiancé," he mumbled.

Suddenly her voice took on a girlish tone. "Oh, Freddie, how wonderful to have his support at this time. Poor, poor, Gretchen. It must have been terrible to watch her go."

Not as terrible as watching you and George running off, Freddie thought.

"Yes, it was, but Patrick – his name's Patrick Nelson by the way – moved in and helped me during the hardest, loneliest days of my life. He'll be staying here for a while, up in Gretchen's room." Her voice choked as she said Gretchen's name.

"Patrick, would you mind taking my sister's things to her room, the blue one, and help her get settled?"

In former days she never would have dared to leave a man alone in her sister's thrall, but life had removed the fangs from this man-eater of old. Freddie now felt pity for her. To think that she had wasted so much emotion, so much pure hate, a hate which was destroying herself more than her sister. As she watched the two of them slowly climb the stairs, she felt as if she were living in a dream. Was it a good dream, or a bad one?

"Have you two been together long?" Al asked. She was panting as she struggled with the steps.

"Just a few months. We met in Hartford, in an art course." Was she, this sad relic of the past, actually attempting to ingratiate herself with him?

8

Goodbye

On that rain-soaked, gray day a large crowd filled the First Lutheran church for Gretchen's memorial. Word of the prodigal sister's return had quickly spread, and the dramatic tension was felt by all as the two women, dressed in black, entered from a door at the side of the altar. They were accompanied by Patrick, who sat between them in the front pew. Gretchen's two nieces and a large group from the Ladies' Guild filled the other seats nearby.

The rest of the mourners were townspeople, most of them curious to view the well known Eliot girls, or "The Boys" as many called them. Who, they wondered, was the nice looking man sitting with them? Surely not the man whom they had fought over, ten years ago.

At Freddie's suggestion (and expense) Al had had a quick rinse job on her graying hair, a facial, and had bought an attractive new dress. The contrast between the sisters was stark. The years had been kind to Freddie, softened her, and made her prettier, while Al's face and stance showed the scars of a hard life.

Originally, Freddie had planned to take over the cooking of the luncheon following the service, but the arrival of Al had changed the picture. It was a great relief to watch the team of churchwomen as they joyfully prepared to honor their old friend.

As expected, most of the mourners came to the house after the ritual. Many of them were driven by curiosity, not hunger. They stared quite openly at the Eliots and the mysterious stranger. Sometimes Al and Patrick had to flee to the privacy of the den, conscious of the intense scrutiny of the guests in the living room. Freddie, as the hostess, should have been the star performer, but Al and Patrick stole the scene.

"My God, sometimes I feel as if I'm being stripped naked, the way this crowd looks us over," laughed Patrick as they found a quiet corner in the room. He had not counted on getting chummy with Freddie's sister, but the inquisitors in the next room had forced it.

Looking at Al, who was sitting on a small couch next to him, he smiled and said, "I don't know what made the change, but you're certainly looking a lot better than when you arrived yesterday."

"Thank you, sir. A back-handed compliment, but I'll take it."

As she smiled at him, he detected a faint trace of the charm she must have had. "My sister's been wonderful to me in every way. I've made a dog's dinner out of my life, and messed up hers, too, but she's forgiven me. Did you know that she's actually made plans for us to go into business together? I guess you know I'm busted." She wanted Patrick's sympathy. "My beloved George trickled away all my money. I really did Freddie a favor when I snatched him away from her."

This was becoming too confessional for Patrick.

"We better get back to the others. God knows what they're saying about us behind our backs." Or did she care, he wondered.

✶ ✶ ✶ ✶ ✶ ✶

"Poor Gretchen," Freddie thought as she moved about the living room, weaving through the crowd. "This is her day, her time in the spotlight, yet her name's been hardly mentioned." Al and Patrick had stolen all the attention.

As she watched the parade of casserole-bearing women, hurrying back and forth from the kitchen, she was glad to have been relieved of catering for the occasion. The stress of her sister's surprise arrival and the problem of making her presentable had been sufficient challenge. Twenty-four hours was hardly enough time to erase years of neglect, but the Al who first appeared at the door and the Al who walked into the service the next day were two different women. Subconsciously, Freddie must not have wanted the world to see that she had been bested by an unattractive rival. Al, the former threat of the past, had vanished forever.

As they talked together, Freddie gradually learned the details of her sister's life – her recent years of financial struggle, and a marriage that Freddie now thanked God to have been spared. How could I have bitten my nails about such a baby-faced twerp, she asked herself. What had both of them seen in such a selfish, spoiled young man? Those eyes, those long lashes, what else? As might be expected, the red-hot romance of the two young people soon fizzled out, as they became bored with each other. After a few months in Cincinnati, George began drinking heavily. He had a rich wife, no job, no need to earn money. Why work, when you could go on cruises, roll dice at the casino, and every few years get a new Jaguar? Eventually the money supply dwindled, unsurprisingly, after months of losing a thousand a night at the tables. George begged his young wife to forgive him, give him one last handout, a chance to make money on his own. He, who was never very bright, was conned into investing in a franchise called "Pampered Poocheria." She really had high hopes for it, Al told Freddie. Then the business, "a spa for pampered pets," was closed down by the local SPCA. The dog groomers were sadistic; the "hotel rooms" were filthy. For Al, this was the finale. She filed for divorce, and returned to her maiden name.

"I was too ashamed to tell anyone about my desperate situation. That kind of pride can kill you. Yet I didn't have enough pride to avoid applying for a job in a strip joint. Would you believe they turned me down because I was too fat?" Yes, I would, thought Freddie, though the picture of Al in such place made her feel sick.

While they talked, Freddie was helping her sister to fasten the pearl necklace that she had lent her to wear at the service. Tearfully, they both remembered the day Freddie had worn her father's gift for the first time. Lending the necklace to Al had been her ultimate act of reconciliation. She began to cry.

"You were thinking of Dad, too, weren't you?" Al comforted her.

"Of him, and of Aunt Gretchen, too," said Freddie. "She was so stoic, so bossy, even at the end. You know, I think she'd be smiling right now if she saw the two of us together."

"I'm glad Dad never knew how I messed up, how I hurt you. It was so good of you to let me wear the necklace." Al embraced her sister.

"Look, dear, let's close the book on that. Let's turn another page, as Patrick would say."

"Speaking of Patrick, what a good man he seems."

"He seems – and is. I'm very lucky," said Freddie. Timing is everything, she thought. Patrick had arrived at the perfect moment in her life. Now Al had arrived. It was much too early to tell what her return might mean to all of them.

9

Planning

Two days later Patrick left. He was no longer needed. The sisters seemed to have reached a state of rapprochement, enjoyed each other's company, and spent hours happily planning their future in business together. Freddie had been enormously relieved to learn that Al was not penniless. Obviously her art course had to be discontinued, and her meetings with Patrick were put on hold.

Before leaving, Patrick had said to Freddie, half jokingly, "Am I still considered your fiancé?"

"Tough question. How do you feel about it?" She kissed him somewhat absentmindedly as they walked down the stairs from Gretchen's room. Her sister's arrival had brought a subtle change in the atmosphere, a cooling in their relationship. "Perhaps we should tread water for a while," she suggested, with a smile.

"Until she moves out?"

That was the big question. Presently, Al had no place to live, and her finances and the settlement of Gretchen's trust were still in limbo. Between them they had two business assets, which they had been discussing. They owned a large and gracious house, and Freddie had a well-known talent as a cook. With Al's help as a hostess, and Freddie's skill in the kitchen, they might transform Eliot Farm into a popular sort of tearoom. Or better yet, a tea*house*, where Freddie's delectable foods could be featured.

The more they talked about it, the more excited they became. As they sat together on an ancient glider on the front porch, they planned how they would furnish it. "This glider has so many memories, but it's got to go. Those ugly little tables, and the rickety rockers, they'll go to the dump, too," the girls decided. "Some really handsome white wicker chairs in Victorian style were being made these days," said Freddie. "We have to keep the Victorian look."

Elegance was the key in planning their new venture. Everything from the furniture, the tea cloths, the English bone china, and the sterling silver had to be first class, no skimping. People would be willing to pay extra for an old fashioned, truly luxurious experience, even in a backwater town like Newfield. Food would be no problem. Freddie's cakes and pies were already known throughout the area.

With a space for about ten tables, the porch would be limited to summer use only, Al had said, but how about a glassed-in porch?

"If we spent that kind of money on it, we'd have to change its name from 'porch' to 'veranda,'" laughed Freddie.

Patrick, who had been sitting in on some of the discussions, suggested local auctions and estate sales as ways to acquire heirloom china at Woolworth prices. "You don't have to have the same patterns on all the tables. Un-matched pieces could be very attractive."

Impulsively, Al reached out and gave his arm a squeeze. Freddie noticed it but was not alarmed. It didn't mean a thing, she told herself. Al had always been a touchy-feely type.

"Patrick, since when have you been an interior decorator? You hardly seem the type!" Al had become much more relaxed and friendly with him in the past few weeks. He was deeply interested in the girls' project, even offering to design a sign for the Eliot Tea House. "Dignified, but not folksy." All agreed that it should be a sophisticated place, a far cry from the "Ye olde tearoom" of former days. No liquor would be served, but in every other way, it should mirror the ambience of a fine restaurant.

Donald Bailey, ever conservative, had some reservations. The Eliot finances had been his concern for years. "Don't go overboard on this 'elegance' kick. I'm sure you'll find many ways to make it attractive without losing your shirts." At the word 'shirts' Al gave him a coy look. She couldn't help herself. Freddie saw it and shrugged it off. Ruefully, she acknowledged that her sister was a born flirt, even in her current condition. She always had automatic reflexes in the presence of a man, and Bailey was a handsome one.

Meanwhile, Freddie was tactfully seeking ways to rehabilitate Al. To be a hostess in their elegant teahouse, Al should look elegant, and in her present chubby state that could be a problem. She was not obese, but she needed to slim down, to return to the chic figure that she once had. Diet, exercise and a shrewd sense of style could do wonders, Freddie thought, as they both signed up for classes at a nearby gym. There was no rush, fortunately, as the money from Gretchen's trust had yet to be distributed. Following their lawyer's advice, the sisters controlled their buying impulses and scanned through decorating and food magazines instead.

Al's idea of enclosing the porch was vetoed for the time being. "Better see how you make out in the summer," Bailey advised. He had not been too optimistic about the sisters' project. They both had enough money to live reasonably well. Why take the risk? Chances were they'd soon be married anyway. That Patrick Nelson looked like a good prospect for Freddie, though Bailey did not like the way Al was looking at him.

✶ ✶ ✶ ✶ ✶ ✶

Curiosity about "The Boys" continued to grow in the town. The prodigal daughter and her sister were watched in the local shops and at the gym. Al worked hard at her exercises and had lost considerable weight, while gaining in vivacity, particularly through her eyes. They now had the old sparkle, but she had a long way to travel before she would regain her crown as Newfield's glamour girl. It was Freddie who was rated the more attractive and interesting of the Eliot girls. Both were often spotted with Patrick, walking with them, arm in arm. He seemed to be giving them equal attention. Watching the trio, some wondered if he really was *Freddie's* fiancé. It was hard to tell.

The gossip grew when the local paper printed details of Gretchen's trust, which had recently been settled. Would the sisters continue living together at the farm, or would Al disappear again?

With most of her chubbiness gone, some wondered if Al would be making a play for Patrick? Old friends of Gretchen's had long memories. Freddie was their favorite. She needed their protection. "Just because a woman loses her looks doesn't mean she's lost her power," they whispered.

The talk stopped when the *Newfield Bee* ran a feature story, headlined *Eliot Sisters to Start New Local Enterprise*. The Eliot Farm, a town landmark, they wrote, "would soon become a fashionable teahouse." The sisters would have preferred the word "elegant" instead of "fashionable" but they were glad to get the publicity. They planned – at a later date – some quarter-page ads with pictures of the house and the Eliot sisters.

10

Progress

In the meantime there was much to do before the opening in May. The old mouse-gray color of the house needed brightening. "No, we don't want chartreuse, or an orangey yellow. Something softer, more between lemon and lime. That way the white fretwork will show up well," Freddie told the painter.

He was not happy. His family had been painting the Eliot house for 40 years. Sometimes they went for brown, sometimes gray, but *yellow*, never. "And as for touching up all of those fancy details in white, it'll bring the cost way up," he warned.

"Trust us, Barney. We really know what we're doing." Al laughed as she charmed him with a smile. "We'll need to do something about those old shutters, too. Do you think we'll need new ones, or could you paint over that dirty white color?"

"Better buy new ones. The old ones ain't worth repairing. You say you want dark green?" He looked unconvinced. Those young Eliot women were attractive, but he wondered about their taste. "I suppose you'll want to change the floor color on the porch?"

"Of course. This old house is going to look so beautiful, no one will believe it. It's going be a showplace, wait and see. You and your family will be our honored guests when our teahouse opens," said Al as she took the old man's arm and led him down the front steps.

She's at it again, thought Freddie as she watched her sister. Charm could be a powerful weapon at times, particularly if you want to lower the cost of something. Why, she mused, did I always end up paying the full price of everything? Too proud to turn on the charm, she guessed.

So it happened that Freddie came up with the ideas, and Al did the negotiating. A very satisfactory system, she thought, as she saw Al smiling at the landscapers as they wandered about the grounds.

"We have loads of wild dogwoods out back, but those old lilacs have got to go. They're all legs and no bloom. I suppose it would cost a fortune to plant hundreds of azaleas, the rose and white ones preferably, around the front of the house?" asked Freddie. Leave it to Al. She'd get a good price.

Freddie's idea of dark green awnings to block the heat on the porch was vetoed. Much too expensive. On the whole, their arguments were easily resolved. It was a happy time for the sisters. And for Patrick, too, who spent most of his weekends helping them with their plans. His idea of visiting auctions and estate sales with them had been very successful. At times they found incredible bargains when they went hunting for fine china or silver. Patrick had found some books on the subject, studied them, and he helped them enormously with his knowledge. He grew even more excited than the girls when they succeeded in acquiring a twelve-piece set of Spode at a price that heartened even their skeptical lawyer.

"When the ladies sip tea from those elegant tea cups they'll forget how much that tea had cost them," Patrick crowed.

"Ladies? What about men? Freddie's cakes and pies should lure the men. We don't want just a bunch of little old ladies coming to our teahouse."

"Al, you're running true to form," laughed Freddie. "Yes, I think my pies and cakes will be appreciated by the men, but I hope the women will order them in advance and bring some goodies home with them."

Her idea of telephone orders turned out to be one of the most successful in the whole operation, and from the opening day on May 5, the public from the entire area responded to the newspaper ads about the *"Special Eliot House Tea. $15.00 a person. Reservations suggested. Pies and cakes may be ordered in advance.* One of the few men in attendance at the opening was Barney Goldsmith, the house painter, who came with three members of his family. They were wearing their churchgoing outfits and did not look too comfortable as they handled, somewhat gingerly, their teacups. Word had gotten out about the high value of the crockery.

Grudgingly Barney admitted to his family, "I didn't think much of those girls' ideas at first, thought they were going a little bit over the top, but look at this crowd. Had to turn away some of them." Overhearing some of the comments about new color scheme of the house, made him almost forget how he had resisted the changes at first. Hadn't his wife often said, "Barney, let the customer make the final choice."

As he bit into a crabmeat sandwich (one of various finger-sized delicacies that were included in the tea menu) Donald Bailey had to admit that the Eliots' fantasies were beginning to come true. There were times when the sisters seemed to be slipping deeper and deeper into debt: the cost of the house painting, the landscaping and the price of all that fancy wicker furniture seemed ridiculous; and even if they had made some shrewd buys at auctions and estate sales, why couldn't they have bought some nice, inexpensive, Japanese cups and saucers, instead of heirloom china, which probably would be shattered by some careless waitress?

As their lawyer, he had approved their sale of 220 acres to a real estate developer who promptly split the property into two acre "pleasure zones." The woods in the back of the Eliot farm were retained as part of a 20-acre buffer between the Eliots and the modern world.

Annie Payson, the long time society editor on the *Bee,* gushed after attending the teahouse opening: *No question about it, the long awaited transformation of the well-loved landmark, the Eliot Farm, into "The Eliot Farm Teahouse" is a whopping success. The Eliot sisters, Alberta and Fredrika, known to most as "Al and Freddie," or simply as "The Boys," have achieved their dream of creating a delightful escape into another world. Those of us who have sipped tea at Brown's in London will feel at home at Eliot's, as they nibble on exquisitely prepared tea cakes or sandwiches. Do make a reservation before you go. It's pricey, but who cares!*

The sale of the land had lifted the sisters from the edge of financial ruin, and the Teahouse soon became more of a hobby than an economic necessity. After that first season in 1981, the idea of glassing in the porch was given up. The summer work was exhilarating enough: Al loved her job as the official greeter, while her sister happily created new delights in the kitchen and supervised her helpers, three Lutheran friends of Gretchen. Serving the tea meant finding attractive young girls with capable hands and good legs. Short black skirts and white blouses were their uniforms, and their hair must be worn short, too. No hairs in the Oolong, girls.

It was Al's job to recruit new waitresses each season. Wholesome good looks, scrubbed faces, and lipstick kept to a minimum were all important. Above all, Al told them, "You may look modern, but use old fashioned manners. Don't chitchat, be fast on your feet, and don't break the china."

The girls adored Al. They found her amusing, although the edict about chitchat had cut down on their tips. Customers seemed to like being very nosy with their waitresses: where do you go to college? Do you have a boyfriend? That sort of stuff. Freddie was also adored by her staff of elderly workers. After all, she was Gretchen's "adopted" child.

11

A New Face

With the approach of winter and two very successful summer seasons behind them, Al decided she needed a change. An old college friend had a small apartment in the "village" section of New York and was looking for a renter. Al was seeking more time in the city for shopping and theatergoing with friends, now that she had some money. The sublet was reasonable, as it should be, for a studio. Its kitchen was a joke, but Al did not plan on cooking. She was looking forward to several months of fun in the city.

When he heard of Al's plan, Patrick asked Freddie "Are you sure you won't be lonely this winter, all by yourself in that big house? I recently heard that a woman I once worked with, Janine Fulton, is now divorced and is looking for a job and a place to live. She could be a kind of companion."

"A companion is what old ladies have." Freddie scoffed. "I'm not at that stage yet!"

"Actually this woman's a whiz-bang typist, could help with your writing and with lots of business chores as well. In fact, she's worked on computers and now that you can buy computers for home use, she could put all of your work on your own computer. She could use Gretchen's old room. Privacy for you both. Why don't I send her around to you? I'd really feel better to know that you were not alone," he urged.

Very reluctantly Freddie consented to see her. The idea of a stranger moving into Gretchen's room sickened her. She did not want to argue with Patrick, however. Neither she nor Al was good at figures. At the rate that the teahouse business was growing a cashier and an accountant might be needed. She still was wary of sharing her house with an unknown woman, but agreed to meet Janine Nelson the following Thursday.

✶ ✶ ✶ ✶ ✶ ✶

"Why should I feel nervous?" thought Freddie as she heard the doorbell. "She's the one being interviewed, not I."

Janine Nelson, a dark-haired, smiling young woman, a few years older than Freddie, was on the doorstep. Her deep blue eyes were alive with intelligence. Her high cheekbones gave her a Slavic look. On Freddie's beauty-judging scale the woman would have rated an eight. Fuller lips would have gained her more points, Freddie thought, but her complexion was near perfect.

Both women stood in the doorway together. It was obvious that each had passed the other's inspection. At Freddie's suggestion they went into the den where Freddie had set out her best teacups and a plate of homemade scones.

"Patrick may have told you that I do some writing. That's the easy part. It's the typing that defeats me. He tells me that you're a great typist – actually he said 'whiz bang' – and I certainly could use help with that. In the summer my sister Al and I run a teahouse . . ."

"Oh, I know all about it. Everybody goes to 'The Boys' for tea," Janine Nelson interrupted.

Normally, Freddie would have resented the interruption, but this one came as a compliment. She was beginning to like the young woman very much.

"For the teahouse we'd probably need help with the financial end, but that's in the future. This winter when I'm alone, Patrick thinks that I'd feel less lonely with say, an assistant as an all-around aid with typing and business chores. Basically, I'm a cook first. A writer second."

As she spoke, Freddie thought, "*I'm* the one who's being interviewed. I don't know a thing about her!" Not to worry. Patrick's recommendation was enough.

Patrick, Janine said, had met her some years ago when both worked briefly in a stockbroker's office. Both had moved to other jobs in Hartford – he to an insurance firm, she to a travel company.

"And you haven't seen him since? He must have been really impressed with you," laughed Freddie. She had already decided that she could be happy sharing her house with Janine . . . for the winter, at least.

Janine looked very pleased when shown Gretchen's old room.

"I love the coziness of this place, and with its separate bath, it would be a perfect spot for me. I promise you I'd try to keep out of your hair. Both of us value privacy, I'm sure. There's only one thing I'd like to work out with you: I have a 75-year-old mother in New York. She's frail and dependent on me. Could I take off three days a month to visit her?"

"No problem," Freddie replied. "By that time both of us would be happy with a change."

Janine was hired for one month on a trial basis. It took less than two weeks for each to become compatible. Janine marveled at Freddie's cooking skills. Freddie watched in awe as Janine brought organization out of the chaos in the office, which was located in one corner of the huge kitchen.

"Not only are you a wizard on the typewriter, but you've brought order into my life. I'll be forever grateful to Patrick for telling me about you. To think how I resisted the idea of an assistant," Freddie sighed.

She had hoped with her sister's absence to see more of Patrick. Ironically, she saw him less often, only once a month, on the three-day weekends that Janine spent in New York. To her surprise, she found that she needed him less. Their nights together in her parents' heirloom bed seemed to have lost some of their ardor. There was warmth but no real sizzle in their romance. Patrick continued to be a comfort to her. They enjoyed each other in a calm fashion, in the manner of old married couples.

"I wonder," Freddie sometimes thought, "if in later years we'll wind up sitting glumly in restaurants, without a word to say to each other. Patrick's a fine man, but do I want to spend the rest of my life with him?"

Al obviously would adore him as a brother-in-law. That was no problem. You had only to see them laughing together, teasing each other, to know how devoted she was to him. However, there was a more serious problem: if she and Patrick were married, would Al move out of the house permanently? After all, she was part owner of the teahouse and its surrounding property. Patrick had a problem too: his two young sons lived in Massachusetts with their mother. The steep alimony and child support bills had forced him to give up his dream of being a graphic artist. Marrying him would only add further complications to his life. Their love had grown stale, yet she still felt a tingle when he was close. That wretched, no-good George of long ago was the only man she truly loved. As she lay awake she tried to calm her churning thoughts by dreaming up amusing anecdotes for her latest column.

12

Rumors

Al had lived in New York for several months. She loved the city. Freddie had gone to New York only once to check out her sister's new apartment. She liked the looks of the building on the outside: it was of rosy colored brick with an unusual edging of white marble around its entrance, which made it stand out among it plain brick neighbors. There were only four tenants in the former private house, one studio apartment on each floor. On her way up to Al's place on the second floor, she encountered a vacant-eyed young woman, who was trying to navigate the stairs. She appeared to have broken the heel of one shoe, which she was holding in one hand. Freddie was about to speak to her, but changed her mind. In New York talking to strangers could be risky, Gretchen often warned her. In fact, simply moving to New York was risky, Freddie thought.

Al's constant vivacity had begun to get on Freddie's nerves, and she was glad for some quiet time. In summer she was able to escape into the kitchen, but in the winter, with the teahouse closed, her sister's peppy personality was overwhelming, so she had encouraged Al to sign the lease, even though, as she told Al, "I don't see how you can survive with that kitchen."

"Quite happily," Al had retorted. "I'm a city person, remember."

Yes, Freddie thought, a city of Cincinnati person. What a tragedy that place had been for her. Oh, well, that was eons ago. Perhaps she might get lucky in New York, meet the right man.

She had been thinking those thoughts when her phone rang. It was Matt, of all people. He was calling to order one pecan pie and her special double chocolate mousse cake for the following Thursday.

"My wife's having a birthday and I want something special for her" he said. "I'll come by and pick it up."

It had been years since she had been alone with Matt and she dreaded it. But business was business.

On Thursday, when he appeared at the back door, Freddie immediately saw that he had grown heavier since their ill-fated evening at Rafters and his features had coarsened, but he still could be called a pleasant looking man. For a crazy second her mind saw him again, his round buttocks in those outrageous silk boxer shorts. She had to turn her back to hide her smile. The specter of that humiliating time was finally exorcised.

Smiling, she asked, "Do you have time for a cup of coffee?"

"Love to. As a matter of fact, I've been wanting to talk to you."

There was a tone in his voice that made her nervous. They sat at the huge kitchen table and made attempts at small talk. It was a strain on both of them.

Looking earnestly at her, he finally said, "Freddie, we've been friends for so long that I feel I have the right, call it the obligation, to tell you this." She had never seen him looking so solemn. "There's been nasty talk about you and your sister. You and Al and your friend, Patrick Nelson."

She laughed nervously. "*Ménage a trois*, perhaps? The three of us are good friends, that's all. Am I going to marry him? A good question. The jury's still out on that one."

Matt remained silent. He was sweating a little.

Freddie challenged him. "You didn't come here just to pick up an order. What's going on, Matt?"

Very hesitantly, Matt explained why he had come to see her. Over the months, he said, rumors have been circulating about Al and her sister's fiancé. Frequently they had been seen together in restaurants and at the theater and at concerts.

"Seen by whom? What are you getting at? They both love music and the theater. What's wrong with that?" She tried to smile, but there was a deep hole inside of her, a pain she hadn't felt since Gretchen's death.

"There's more," Matt continued, as Freddie poured him another cup of coffee. "Those college friends of hers who live nearby have seen a tall, curly haired man, leaving her building."

"Ridiculous. New York's full of tall, curly haired men. Look at you. With a little more hair, you could fill that description." She attempted to joke and failed. "Who are these so-called pals, and why are they spreading such malice? I'd have to see a picture to believe them."

"I'm in New York all the time on business. I can get you a picture. What's her address? I have a friend who does a little private investigation on the side."

When Matt finally left, Freddie went into the bathroom and threw up. Freddie usually avoided confrontations.

✳ ✳ ✳ ✳ ✳ ✳

Even when she saw the photo of Patrick walking down the marble steps of Al's building she remained silent, praying that she was living in a bad dream, a dream that would vanish when she awakened. She kept calm. Why stir up trouble?

There was no point in telling Janine about the situation. Freddie's hurt was so deep that confiding in someone would simply add another dimension to her grief. She did not want any pitying words or looks from Janine.

She worked hard on her cooking column, walked the streets of Newfield, trying to fend off questions about her plans: were she and Patrick really engaged? Would he join her in the business if they married? Would her sister continue as her partner? Was it true that Patrick had just been transferred to Chicago?

13

A Simmering Pot

Al returned to Newfield on May 1 for the 1983 season opening of the teahouse. Janine had proved to be so helpful that Freddie asked her to stay on at the farm. More than ever, Freddie needed a friend as well as a very competent assistant. Over the winter Janine had convinced Freddie that one of the new home computers would not only make bookkeeping easier, but she could write her cooking articles on it as well.

Since Patrick's absence the rumors and the inquisitive questions had subsided. If there was any friction between the sisters it was not noticed. Both were too busy getting set for another successful season: hiring helpers on the grounds and in the kitchen and recruiting a new crew of waitresses.

A snowy winter had produced unusually showy blooms on the azaleas and rhododendrons and in the woods behind the house the lacy whiteness of the dogwoods glimmered. Never had the place looked more beautiful; never had Freddie felt more sorrowful and angry. She was angrier with herself than at her sister. How could she have been so blind to the growing electricity between Al and Patrick? All the signs were there: the little pats, the sudden hugs, the secret jokes between them, the possessive way she held his arm, or plucked a hair off his jacket.

Patrick's name was rarely spoken. That in itself should have alerted others that all was not well between the sisters. Outwardly, the coolness between them was well disguised. Al, with energy more dynamic than ever, drilled her new waitresses without mercy.

"Watch it going through the doors. Grip your tray tightly. Set those cups down with reverence and pour the tea as if it were molten gold." (In other words, girls, you're dealing with expensive stuff. Handle with care.)

She also supervised the gardeners as they added ever more plants to the grounds, and she oversaw the installing of new rose-colored awnings over the porch. (Freddie had wanted green, but was overruled. "Rose is more welcoming, warmer," Al had said.)

In the kitchen, the Lutheran ladies were too happy and busy to notice that "The Boys" never spoke to each other, and that after work in their own zones of activity and a pick-up supper on a tray, they each retired to their separate bedrooms. If Janine sensed the coolness between the sisters she was too tactful to mention it. She had not met Al until recently. Though pleasant to each other there was a hint of jealousy between them. She, too, retired to her upstairs bedroom when her office chores were done.

Before his move to Chicago Patrick had phoned both of the sisters and it was obvious that he was secretly relieved to disentangle himself from a sticky situation. "It's a great opportunity, and while I'll miss you both, I can't afford to turn it down."

Miss you *both*, how right he was, thought Freddie bitterly. Strangely enough, it was not Patrick who stoked her growing rage. She should have noticed months ago that he was slipping into an emotional chasm. When queried about his absence, she had a stock answer, "I miss Patrick terribly of course. We all do. He's been such a help launching the teahouse. Marriage? Oh, no, we never thought seriously about it."

"The Hell you didn't," Matt thought. At times he regretted that he had brought things to such a boil. He had been true to his word with Freddie: never did he gossip about her troubles. Only his friend, the investigator, the man whose camera caught Patrick in New York, was privy to the situation. He could be trusted.

If Freddie was heartbroken, she was too proud to show it, but as she watched Al laughing and joking with the customers, she often felt like shouting, "This is the charming bitch who's tricked me again." Instead, she smiled at the guests and said, "Isn't she a hoot! Aren't I lucky to be her sister?"

She was well aware that Al's bubbly personality was as vital to the success of the teahouse as her own famous cooking. Did people come again and again for Freddie's delectable, paper-thin watercress sandwiches and her wonderful hazelnut torte, or were they bewitched by Al's magic rapport with every guest? She made everyone feel important. There were other means to distract her from such self-destruction, however – her growing "take out" business, and a cooking column that she hoped would soon be syndicated. Those interests kept her so engrossed that at times she actually forgot to be angry.

Forgot, that is, until Al on a midsummer evening confronted her in the kitchen, where she was sitting at her desk.

"Freddie, I think it's about time we stopped pussyfooting around the subject that's come between us – Patrick. I talked with him recently, and he wants me to join him in Chicago. Don't look so shocked. There's no point in pretending that things can go on like this."

Stunned and furious, Freddie could barely understand the words that followed. It seems that Al had long been prepared for the confrontation, had even talked it over with Donald Bailey for legal advice.

"I know we're co-owners of everything – house, property and assets, but I'm willing to sell you my share," she said.

"Sell you my share!" What incredible condescension and nerve. "I suppose you've already figured out a price? Something as outrageous as everything else you've done to me!" Freddie flung some papers off her desk and stalked out.

A silent week passed as the sisters grimly went about their work. The young waitresses noticed how much more exacting Al was with them, and how her usually friendly manner with the guests had become almost chilly. Even the customers noticed it.

"Is Al feeling well?" Janine asked Freddie. "She seems sort of edgy, high strung."

"Yes," Freddie agreed. "Frankly, I'm concerned about her. You know our mother died very young, of a heart attack. I'm going to try to get her to take it easier."

The helpers in the kitchen had also noticed the growing tension between the sisters, but they were worried about Al in particular. At their urging, Al finally agreed to rest in the den after work. Very pleased, the women went into a downstairs storage closet, and returned with an old afghan, which they tucked around her as she rested on the couch. Before they went back to their chores in the kitchen they were relieved to see Al peacefully at rest, her eyes closed. Two hours later, with their clean-up work finished, the three elderly cooks tiptoed into the den to check on Al. She was lying motionless, exactly as they had left her, the afghan still tucked around her, but her eyes, those famous violet blue eyes, were wide open, as if staring. She was dead. No question about it.

Ethel, the elder of the three, quickly closed Al's eyes before shouting for Freddie, who ran down immediately. She looked pale and grim as she passed her hand over her sister's brow, then dialed 911.

"This is Fredrika Eliot at Eliot Farm. We've just found my sister Alberta." Her voice shook as she continued. "It looks as if she'd had a heart attack. No, she's not breathing. Please, please hurry."

While she was phoning, Janine had come downstairs. She seemed as pale and shaken as Freddie when she saw Al on the couch. Embracing Freddie, she said, "Dear, how terrible for you. You'd just been saying how worried you were about your sister's heart. And look what's happened." Neither she nor Freddie wept.

Within minutes an ambulance and police car arrived at the house.

The five women clung to each other, too stunned to speak. Freddie and Janine remained silent while the elderly women wept. It was Janine who answered the policemen's questions.

"No, she didn't seem ill, just over tired. Heart problems run in her family, and we all were worried about her, begged her to take it easy."

"Ladies, I would suggest that you go into the next room and try to rest while Tim and I have some routines to go through and some calls to make," said Howard Close, the senior of the two officers.

"Those calls, could they mean you'll need a coroner?" Freddie's voice shook as she said "coroner." Her hand trembled as she laid it on the policeman's shoulder and anxiously looked into his face.

"Don't upset yourself about that, Miss. No need for that. In a sudden death like this there's always an examination to make and a lot of forms to fill out. The ambulance driver and the two of us can manage it ourselves without causing you any more grief than necessary."

Janine tried to console Freddie. "It's horrible enough, dear, without having to deal with a coroner. Don't worry, these kind men want to help you."

The men waited until the women left the room before they drew aside the afghan from Al's body.

Even in death, Al had the power to draw admiration from men. Tim Dorrance, the other officer, said under his breath, "This young woman was really stacked!"

Their ten-minute examination over and all forms filled out and proper authorities notified, the policemen drove back to the station. Their inspection had shown nothing to warrant any suspicion of foul play, but one question stayed in Tim Dorrance's mind: why had the sister showed so much concern about a coroner? Was she afraid of an autopsy? The case worried him, but there were no obvious signs of foul play. Alberta Eliot just looked too young and healthy – and beautiful – to die.

14

Al's Memorial

As expected, a large crowd had come to Al's memorial service. Patrick had arrived that day and sat in the front pew with Freddie. Gossips noted that the pair did not sit close together, and that Patrick did not go back to the house for the reception.

"I was so glad that at least he could get to the church," Freddie explained. "He was lucky to get that much time off from his work." She tried to sound convincing, but failed.

Again, the Lutheran ladies took charge of the feast, though this time Freddie would have welcomed an excuse to escape from the stares of the curious.

Every one marveled at her composure. All of a sudden she had lost everything – her sister, her fiancé and her business, and there she was, standing at the door, calmly welcoming her guests. Only Donald Bailey knew of Al's threat to quit the teahouse and join Patrick. Desperately, Freddie fought her impulse to run far, far away, but she kept on smiling, smiling, until the last guests left. Two of her old friends had offered to spend the night with her, but to their surprise, she declined.

"You're sweet to ask, but right now, I need some quiet time. I guess you could say I'm still in shock. Remember, I have Janine Nelson living with me now. She's been rock solid. I can't think how I could manage without her."

15

Renewal

The death of Alberta Eliot had also meant the death of the teahouse. However, Freddie, after allowing some weeks to pull herself together after Al's death, re-opened her take-out business. Customers still came to the farm to buy her well-known cakes and pies. Some visitors came during the dogwood season to enjoy a walk through the woods, which had been one of the pleasures after having tea at "The Boys."

The woods were located at some distance from the rear of the house. Many of the strollers were relieved to avoid seeing a very depressing sight – the front porch, now neglected and bare, a remnant of happier days. On the lawn, near the entrance the teahouse sign still remained, but was beginning to peel. Freddie had not had the heart to remove it, even now, three years after Al's death.

The closing of the teahouse had not meant a period of leisure for Freddie. She was working frantically, not for the money, there was plenty of that, but for a need to regain her confidence. Her sister's treachery had been forgiven once, but to have been made a fool of twice, was too much. She had been stupid enough to believe that Al, overweight and down-at-the heels, was no longer a threat. Stupidest move of all, she mused, was to pair her off with Patrick, and to be happy that they hit it off so well. Was it entirely Al's fault? Perhaps not. Some women can't help themselves when it comes to men. Well, that was past history. Now it was time for her to mend the cracks in her ego and emotions.

The surprising success of the teahouse had brought her a certain celebrity as a cook, and later as a writer, and she was determined to advance in both careers. Already esteemed for her baking, she enrolled in a special course for making bridal cakes. It was exacting, exciting, creative work and she loved it. She still had time to plan a cookbook, "*Adventures in the Kitchen*," as well as her regular cooking column in the local paper.

It was gratifying to her to feel so competent, but her friends worried about her. Ellen Brown, one of her oldest friends, told her, "Freddie, you're burning yourself out. God knows you don't need the money."

Her friends also worried about her on a more serious level. As one who had gone for years without drinking so much as a thimble of alcohol, she was sometimes seen at the local liquor store ordering cheap wine by the jug. "I need a lot for my cooking," she would say, defensively. The little broken veins in her face said differently.

Some of the sherry did go into her cooking, but a lot of it went down Freddie's throat. She and Janine had grown into the habit of relaxing in the den each evening after work. Sherry had never been classed as a "real drink" in Freddie's mind. It was something sipped by old ladies, she thought. Something quite harmless. "After an exhausting day's work, I really earned this," she would say to Janine as she poured herself another small glassful. The small glasses also made her feel more innocent about her drinking.

During the day both women worked extremely hard. Neither seemed affected by the tipsy hours of the night before. Freddie drank most of the wine. Janine did not get drunk. She calmly listened as Freddie rambled on about her fears and failures. In the mornings Freddie often worried that she had been too open with her confidences.

"Did I make too much of an idiot of myself last night?" she would ask the next day.

"Of course not, dear. You've got a lot of worries on your plate. Leave them off on me. That's what a friend's for." Janine would reply.

Janine was more to Freddie than a confidante. Every day she showed herself to be a remarkable aid. Though the bookkeeping chores involved with the operation of the teahouse no longer were needed, Janine made herself useful in many important ways.

Sitting at her desk in one corner of the kitchen, Janine answered the phone, wrote down orders for "take outs," and worked on the correspondence between Freddie and her sometimes demanding and impatient editor. At times, when Freddie was unusually busy, Janine even did some of the cooking.

"How did you ever learn how to cope with that damned computer?" Freddie would ask as she watched Janine swiftly tapping on the keyboard.

"Easy. I did it for years at work," she smiled. " It's just a matter of practice. Actually, it's much easier than toiling away on a typewriter. Someday you'll be able to compose your thoughts on the computer and save yourself a lot of time. Meanwhile, let me help you. I may not be a very creative writer, but I'm meticulous. Maybe I could save you from making a lot of booboos," laughed Janine.

Spelling was not one of Freddie's strong points, and her punctuation and syntax were questionable. Bit by bit, each learned from the other's expertise. Janine grew more at home in the kitchen, and Freddie now wrote without fear of making of making stupid errors. Most important, Freddie grew less dependent on alcohol as her tension lessened. Friends had noticed this when they dropped in.

"Her face has filled out, and those little veins on her nose have almost gone," they told each other. Janine, they agreed, had turned Freddie's life around.

16

Revelations

The one-month tryout had stretched into seven successful years as Freddie became more and more dependent on her friend, Janine. An office had been built into one corner of the kitchen. Answering mail, paying bills and mailing checks to suppliers and charities kept Janine at the desk for hours. To keep her hands from getting too rough Janine kept a jar of her favorite skin cream right at her desk and always applied it just before she would begin work. It was the same cream she used at night to maintain her perfect complexion. Freddie had long ago gotten used to its pungent odor and hadn't given it a thought in years.

One day Freddie, who had become even more absent-minded as she grew older, said "You know, you do almost everything for me except breathe. I think it's time for you to have power of attorney."

Donald Bailey, who was still her lawyer, had met Janine and had been impressed by her, but was uncomfortable to see the dominance the older woman had upon his client. Yes, Freddie was indeed growing more careless and forgetful, yet she was still alert, and capable. After all, hadn't she published several cookbooks? And, she wasn't even 40.

When the two women appeared in Bailey's office Freddie said, "I'm feeling wonderful right now, but, in case I became ill or lose my marbles, it would be a comfort to know that someone as honest and capable as Janine could handle things for me," she said, smiling, one arm around her friend's shoulder.

"Yes, that makes sense," Bailey had agreed, as they signed the papers. Some months later when Freddie, on another visit (alone) to his office wanted to make Janine her sole heir, he was concerned and successfully convinced Freddie to put off any changes to her will "for now." There was something about Janine that made him uneasy.

Freddie's banker, Stanley Warner, had similar misgivings. When advised of Janine's appointment as power of attorney he had talked to her.

"Naming your friend, Janine Fulton, frankly makes me a little nervous. She will now have total control over your finances. You wouldn't have given her that power unless you had complete trust in her, but as I look over your bank statements, there are certain items that cause me concern."

"Like what?" she challenged.

"Like monthly payment of three thousand dollars to a certain Linda Sherman. Who is this person?"

None of your business, she thought, but answered, "Linda is an elderly, needy woman of 82. She happens to be Janine's mother."

"And do you know this woman?"

"What are you saying? That this could be some kind of a con job?" Freddie was furious.

"Of course not, but people like you, kindly people, can be victimized."

Freddie decided to lie. "I met this poor woman, and believe me, I wish I could help her more." Actually, she also had been suspicious at first, but couldn't bring herself to question her friend's honesty.

The banker continued, "There are two other monthly payments that I'm curious about – these are lesser amounts, but the names of the organizations aren't familiar to me. Three hundred dollars a month is made out to *Open Door* and to another called *A Day in the Country*. Are you sure that these so-called charities are on the up and up?"

Freddie was growing more and more angry.

"Just because you haven't heard of them doesn't mean they aren't legit. You should read the grateful letters that come to us."

She did not want to admit that in recent years she'd come to depend totally on Janine in handling her finances. Freddie rarely opened her own checkbook or looked at her bank statements. It was a Godsend to have a friend like Janine.

As she stood up to leave she said bitterly, "Stanley, you've made me very upset by all this distrust. If my account is too much trouble for you, I can take it elsewhere."

The Eliot family account had for 50 years been one of the small bank's most prestigious assets. Stanley smiled grimly as he shook her hand and led her to the door. "Sorry, Freddie, I was just trying to protect your interests."

When Janine heard about the encounter she was not surprised.

"Of course, dear, he's worried about you. That's his job. The *Open Door* and *A Day in the Country* are small potatoes, compared to the big outfits like the Red Cross and the Salvation Army, but they're perfectly legitimate. I wouldn't be helping them myself if I didn't trust them."

A few days later a later from Stanley Warner arrived.

Dear Freddie,

> Regarding our conversation the other day: I checked out the two charities, Open Door and A Day in the Country and they are absolutely legitimate. Guess I made a fool of myself. Sorry!
>
> Cordially,
> Stanley

Gleefully, Freddie showed the letter to Janine.

✱ ✱ ✱ ✱ ✱ ✱

Some time ago, when Janine had first mentioned the two charities to Freddie, she too had been dubious about them. "Why do you suggest that I give to them?" she had asked.

"Because I'm on the board of both of them, and I know the good work they do. Why don't we go down to their offices and check them out," Janine suggested.

Their "offices" situated in a seedy building downtown did little to calm Freddie's misgivings. Both were located next to each other and were equally unimpressive: a couple of desks, a table, bulletin boards and a few chairs were the furnishings. The staff, she was told, was made up of volunteers. Nobody was at hand in either office.

Janine explained, "We don't operate full time, except for collecting the mail, which I do, as treasurer. It's a two-bit operation, I admit, but in our small way we do help others." She went on to describe how the *Open Door* was a charity founded to help the poor and the elderly in nursing homes. Twice a year Christmas gifts and birthday presents were distributed by their organization to those with special needs. "We don't give elaborate gifts, but when you consider the number of patients in those places, the figures can mount up." As she spoke she opened a file of letters from grateful recipients.

The second organization, she said, was created by her and others to give city children four gala picnics in the country each summer. She was also the treasurer, and her duty was to collect mail donations and bank them.

"If you could see the expressions on those kids' faces when they board the buses and set off for a wonderful day in the country, you'd reach for your checkbook," she said. On a large bulletin board along the dingy wall she pointed out the pictures of hundreds of grinning children.

After that first visit Freddie made a modest contribution to both charities and had been gradually increasing her donations each year. She had always given generously to the major organizations, but she never had the emotional attachment that she had with "Janine's charities" as she called them. The outings for children had special appeal for her.

17

Paranoia

One May day in 1990 as she and Janine strolled through the property, Freddie exclaimed, "Look at those dogwoods! Have you ever seen them looking so beautiful!"

Janine laughed. "Dear, you say the same thing every year."

"I've just had an idea, such an obvious one that I wonder why we didn't think of it before. We have these lovely woods right here. Why not use them for next spring's picnic? Ten acres should be enough to contain 120 kids. What do you think?"

"What a great idea! Let's get working on it right away," exclaimed Janine. Actually the idea of using the Eliot woods had been in her mind for a long time, but she had hesitated to bring up the subject with Freddie. Over the years she had learned to make Freddie believe that all the good ideas were hers alone. Above all, Janine knew that Freddie must never fear that she was losing control, which, of course, she was.

The monthly payments to the mysterious Linda Sherman continued. As time passed, the checks grew larger. It seemed as if Mrs. Sherman lived from crisis to crisis as more and more money was needed: one month there was a hip operation; another month dentures must be replaced; another month her apartment was ransacked and burglarized. Freddie was always there to rescue her.

"Wouldn't it make more sense if you simply moved in with her and took care of her?" she once asked Janine. (It was a risky question. God knows how I could manage without her, she thought.)

"Sounds logical, but the problem is we just don't get along," Janine confessed. "Three days with Mom is all I can take. Freddie, you're incredibly generous and trusting. For all you know, Linda Sherman may be just a sham."

"Do you have a picture of her? Is she some gray-haired, fragile old lady, with a sweet, dimpled face? Or is she a sharp-tongued old hag?"

In a rare moment of confidence, Janine said, "For most of my life, my mother was a mess. She drank, she played around (my father left her for that reason) she served time for shoplifting. She was, as they say, a 'nasty piece of business.'"

Freddie was shocked. "And yet you forgave her?"

"Well, life has softened her now, and me, too. I guess I've learned forgiveness, the hard way."

As she looked at the calm expression on her friend's face, Freddie wondered if she could ever reach that serenity. Could she ever forgive her sister? How does one learn forgiveness?

One night, during her drinking period, Freddie had spent a long hour of drunken confessions with her new friend, Janine. She had little memory of those tipsy words, but feared ever since that she had said far too much, had unveiled too many of her secrets. How much of her story had she told – her bitter quarrel with her sister, the details of Al's betrayals, first with George, later with Patrick? What had she confessed about Al's death – that she might have caused it by her refusal to allow her to quit the business and follow Patrick to Chicago? It was unfortunate that she had exposed her anxieties to Janine. Now Janine had emotional power as well as financial power over her. It was an uncomfortable feeling, a sense of being vulnerable, as if Janine were standing over her, holding a big stick, which she could use whenever it suited her.

18

The Picnic

One day as she was rolling out the pastry for a pecan pie order, Freddie said to Janine. "You really think that I could learn to forgive? I still can't get the bitterness out of my soul whenever I think about my sister."

"I was thinking about her recently, how she died so young. My own heart, at 41, isn't what you'd call perfect. Years ago I was laid up for nine months with a rheumatic heart condition," said Freddie. "But let's get off this dreary subject. It's time to think about the picnic. How many apple pies do you think we'll need?"

✶ ✶ ✶ ✶ ✶ ✶

It was a glorious spring day at Eliot Farm, but Janine and Freddie were far too busy to notice the whitening petals of the dogwoods in the woods or the thousands of daffodils, which seemed to have blossomed overnight. Two weeks was barely enough time to complete the plans for the gala picnic on May 15. Janine and her volunteer committee were on the telephone checking on all the non-food problems: hiring the three buses, going over all the lists of participating children, recruiting two chaperones for every bus, and most important of all, raising additional funds for emergencies. (Last year the rising price of bus rentals had created a crisis.)

"Don't forget to include a doctor among the chaperones. Remember how Roger Hammonds broke a leg on the August outing? What a hassle that was. Fortunately, some of us had cars that day, so we got him to the hospital. At least we won't have that problem here. Southdown Hospital is just a few minutes away," said Susan Kenyon, a dedicated, but somewhat neurotic, member of the committee.

Freddie and three others in the cooking group were discussing the menu for the event. The ubiquitous hot dogs and rolls would be purchased, but the rest of the feast would be homemade: potato salad, the standard kind; hard-boiled eggs, tossed salads and chili. Freddie volunteered to provide the dessert, as usual.

"Making pies and brownies for more than 130 people, are you sure you can do it, Freddie?"

"Trust me, girls. I'm a pro, remember?" She smiled, but deep down, she was a bit nervous. The brownies could be baked some days in advance, wrapped in foil, and stored. Baking all those pies would be a challenge, but they could be frozen, she decided. Normally, she would never serve a frozen pie to anyone. Short cuts were against her religion (and so were hot dogs). She was exhilarated by the thought of opening her woods for the annual outing and remembered how, as a child, she had been so joyful as she ran through the trails during the dogwood season. For generations the Eliot family had picnicked in those woods, and years ago Patrick had built, with much care, a large brick barbeque.

Would it be adequate for such a crowd, she wondered? "I think we should bring some portable grills, otherwise we'd be all day grilling those damned hot dogs, and the kids won't have time for play," she said.

"You're such a crank about frankfurters, Freddie," said one of her friends. "What is it that you hate about them?"

"First of all, their looks. Can you think of anything more unattractive? Don't tempt me to tell you what they remind me of. Secondly, I can't believe that all that garbage they put into them can be any good for you. Does that answer your question, or should I confess the real truth: I'm a food snob, or hadn't you guessed?"

✶ ✶ ✶ ✶ ✶ ✶

Everyone agreed that the outing to Eliot Farm was the best ever. The weather was perfect – cloudless, crisp enough to be invigorating, but not chilly. For once, the bus company had sent new vehicles, and they arrived on time. A record number of children were counted, and none unaccounted for. (On other trips some had strayed in the woods and caused panic until they were found.) Nobody was hurt, not even a grazed knee. Every morsel of food was eaten. No extra work for the clean-up crew. It had been an exhausting day, but a very happy one.

Only one incident had annoyed Freddie. Jim Bankson, who had volunteered at the grill, ran a very successful real estate firm in town. He could not resist nagging Freddie on his favorite topic, the Eliot acreage. Like many top realtors he worked nonstop, even when he was supposed to be having fun. If he had not been a pal of Janine's, she would have cut him off rudely, instead she tried to jolly him off the subject.

"Jim, as a dedicated real estate salesman, you can be a real pain in the butt. How many times have I told you that I don't want to sell off any more land? And stop looking so lustfully at my woods!"

At an earlier time Janine, too, had mentioned disposing of some of the property. Freddie's immediate anger was a shock to her.

"What a ridiculous idea! You and your friend, Jim, must be cooking up some deal. Sorry, I didn't mean to offend you, but you know how I feel about this land, especially the woods. Consider the subject closed."

19

Fire

The next morning both women slept late. Freddie was suddenly awakened by the screaming sirens of fire trucks that seemed as if they were right in her bedroom. Looking out her bedroom window she saw men shouting and running with hoses in the direction of the woods, which were ablaze.

She rushed downstairs, half dressed, and shouted to the firemen, "Good God, what happened?"

"Lady, we don't know. Must have been some carelessness after the picnic."

In dismay, she cried, "It couldn't have been. The place was perfect when we left it." She began to weep and couldn't stop. Her woods, her beloved dogwoods would soon be ashes.

In vain, Janine tried to comfort her. They stepped outside and watched as the firemen dragged their hoses closer to the flames. It was almost a hopeless cause – the hoses were too short, the water pressure too weak to save all of the woods.

When it was over, the men gathered in the kitchen for some coffee and cake. Freddie was still in tears as she and Janine served them. Exhausted and frustrated, some of the men also seemed puzzled.

"Did you notice," mused one of them, "the strongest flames were in the middle of the woods. They seemed to be moving in a straight line, from east to west, almost as if some one had poured something." He stopped. This could be arson – better not discuss it.

✶ ✶ ✶ ✶ ✶ ✶

The fire at Eliot Farm made the front page of the paper the next day. Not that it was a huge conflagration: only a part of the woods was destroyed, but the story had so many elements of interest. First, anything connected with the Eliot family piqued the town's curiosity. Second, how did that fire get started? Were the rumors about an arson investigation true? Third, what would the "heart-broken" owner, Fredrika Eliot, do next?

She was much too distraught to make any plans. The idea of arson was too shocking to contemplate. Who, and why, would anyone want to do such a thing? She, and all those involved with the picnic, had been queried by the investigators. Their answers were always the same: no, all fires were carefully put out before we left, and all picnic debris gathered up, no papers on the ground, and of course, no cigarettes. (Not many smoked these days.)

Sometimes Freddie tried to persuade herself that lightning had caused the fire, but lightning would never have caused the flames to burn in such a strange manner, racing along in a straight line. Unfortunately, arson seemed to be the only answer. A thin line of unscathed dogwoods remained, but just a few yards away, a wide expanse of charred trees and sooty black soil could be seen, a sight which made her weep. The magic that the place once held for her was gone forever. Perhaps it was time to think about selling some of her acreage.

20

Land for Sale

When she went to visit Bailey at his law office Freddie did not tell Janine about it. In doing so, she felt a twinge of guilt. She and Janine had always acted together, but this time she felt a need to talk to her lawyer alone.

"Donald," she said, as she sat in an easy chair in his oak-paneled room, "I'm in a quandary, as you can imagine. I loved that stretch of woods, as you know, and I always resisted selling it, but right now, I can't even bear to look at it. For ages Janine has urged me to sell. She says the land is worth a lot of money."

Bailey was discreetly silent. He raked his fingers through his white hair and looked at his client over the rims of his half-glasses. Ever since the fire he had been expecting her visit. The fact that she had come alone, had escaped her Svengali-like companion, was of great interest. His initial distrust of Janine had grown even more intense since the destruction of the woods. Janine and Jim Bankson were often seen at the diner, having coffee together. Right now they were probably dreaming up ways to lure Freddie into selling the property. Janine would get a handsome kickback, he was sure.

"Does Janine know you're here?" he asked.

She reddened before answering. "No. I feel a little funny, sort of sneaky, about coming to see you alone like this. It isn't as if I didn't trust her but, I just had to get another opinion before I made a move."

"Before you sell, is there any way that the burnt out areas could be reclaimed?"

"It would take too many years. In any case, my love for those woods has gone. You could say it's like seeing the scarred face of a person you've once loved. The feeling's dead. If there's going to be a sale, I want to make it through you."

And not Janine, he thought. How very interesting. Leslie Jenks, a woman client of his, and a broker in a rival firm of Jim Bankson's, could handle the deal. He picked up his phone. "Connect me with Leslie Jenks of Country Realty, please."

✶ ✶ ✶ ✶ ✶ ✶

A week later, a round faced, smiling woman, rang the bell at Eliot Farm. She introduced herself and handed her a card. "Hi, I'm Leslie Jenks, from Country Realty. A few days earlier she had called Freddie, saying "Donald Bailey said you might be interested in selling some land. I assume it's the property that was recently involved in a fire? Would it be possible for me to look at it?" Freddie and Leslie found a mutually satisfactory date and the appointment was made.

Freddie was relieved that Janine was not home as they walked towards the woods. She had never told her about the conversation with Donald Bailey. It was rather refreshing to be doing something on her own, a sort of freedom which she had not felt for years.

Though the damage to the property had been shown in the papers, Jenks was shocked when she saw it. "What a terrible thing to have happened. You must feel devastated," she said.

"More than that. I've lost a chunk of my childhood. How I loved those woods," Freddie answered, almost on the point of crying.

After the short inspection they sat together in the kitchen. Janine had gone into New York to visit her mother, so Freddie did not feel a sense of pressure to make the woman leave. Price was not discussed. Three members of her firm would arrive at a figure once they had made a more complete inspection of the land, she was told. As Janine would not return for two days, Freddie hoped that they could move fast.

"Could they possibly come tomorrow?" she asked.

She was in luck. The brokers arrived the following day and ten acres of the Eliot Farm were officially listed for sale.

21

Reluctance

A heavy rain, two days after the fire, had wrecked the investigators' chances of making progress in their search for evidence of arson. Any evidence that might have been there had been washed away, but rumors remained, particularly after it became known that the property was on the market. In real estate circles there had long been gossip about building a strip mall in the area. The Eliot acres, in size and shape, would be perfect.

Freddie's reaction when she heard the rumors was predictable. She was almost as heartsick as she had been after the fire. She did not discuss the rumors with Janine. There had been a coldness between them ever since Janine learned about the listing with Country Realty. Freddie had not had the courage to tell Janine about it when she returned from New York. It was Jim Bankson who broke the news to her as they had their usual coffee break at the diner.

"We got skunked, gal. That bitch pulled a fast one. Went to Bailey, who had a contact with Leslie Jenks. Why, that woman hasn't made a decent sale in her life. Funny thing, though, she'll probably make a few bucks out of it, even if she doesn't know what she's doing."

Janine shrugged. "Well, we tried, Jim. God knows we put the pressure on her for years. Maybe we tried too hard, turned her off. Most of the time I can handle her, but this time she got stubborn. I have to live with her, so I guess I'll just have to play dumb for a while."

"And for you, dear, that ain't easy," Jim said as they walked out.

✶ ✶ ✶ ✶ ✶ ✶

Despite a boom in real estate values, selling the Eliot acres was not as simple as Leslie Jenks had hoped. Could it be that people were superstitious about "unlucky" property? The Eliot family's ill-fated lives had become legend in the area. Accident-prone was the label. As the weeks and months passed with little activity, Leslie became depressed. What about that shopping mall rumor?

Leslie had been given an exclusive listing. Perhaps she should share it with another agency? But just as she was at her lowest confidence level she got lucky and sold the land to a big developer from Boston. Yes, he told her, after strolling through the sad remains of the woods, the Eliot acres would be ideal for a modest sized shopping mall. The bulldozers could begin right after the final closing, he said.

Meanwhile Freddie had been praying for a miracle. She thought about dividing the land into two-acre parcels, enough space to build five attractive houses. She toyed with planting tall arbor vitaes along her property line. Expensive, yes, but the screening would be worth it. In her imagination she visited her possible new neighbors, making pleasant new friends. She was beginning to feel almost happy about the prospect, when she got the call from her broker.

"I have great news for you. We have a buyer, Leon Drake, from Boston. No haggling, he'll pay full price."

Leon Drake was a familiar name to Freddie. He had created many of the shopping malls that were despoiling the New England suburbs. Her spirits sank.

"Well, I don't know. The idea of a mall so close to my house appalls me."

The broker was desperate, and pushed on. "I've seen the plans and they're surprisingly attractive. He wants to create a sort of garden setting. Lots of attractive trees and bushes. Might even retain some of the dogwoods, or plant arbor vitae along the borders, as you once thought of doing. Would you care to look at the plans? I'll bring them to you."

Very reluctantly, Freddie agreed to meet with Leslie to look at the plans. The low, flat-roofed buildings would be unobtrusive, she admitted, if screened as planned, and the whole project was on a modest scale. Her price had been met without a quibble. No other offer had been made. After conferring with Bailey, the deal was done.

When the sale price was reported in the paper, Janine said scornfully, "Why, Jim could have gotten you triple for that. Developers would kill for such a property."

"Then why did it take so long to sell, even at that price?" said Freddie irritably. "I think you're choking on sour grapes."

"A smart realtor would have handled it much better. In any case, the sale may hit a few bumps in the road when it goes before the zoning board. Another thing: what about an access road to the property. How are the customers going to reach this wonderful mall? By helicopter?" Janine said sarcastically.

"I think Donald Bailey's got it under control. He has enormous clout with the zoning people, and as for the access road, he has something worked out that will more than make up for what you call a 'low price.' Let's change the subject."

Freddie's mood was as black as the charred remains of the woods

The Zoning Board did wilt before the combined power of Donald Bailey and the developer's lawyers. Later, an agreement was reached about an access road, which pleased everybody: by giving up a two-acre sliver of land on the far edge of the farm to be used as access, Fredrika Eliot was to "receive two percent of the future leases on the stores." Naturally, Bailey would receive a cut, but he deserved it, Freddie thought.

To top it all, she would still retain more than eight acres of privacy.

22

Getting Away

"Eliot Woods" was the name of the projected mall. An ironic title, Freddie thought, as she tried to shut out the noise of the bulldozers, which had been tearing up the earth for weeks. She sighed as she saw the last of the dogwoods being plowed under. So much for the proposed plan to save them. She hadn't waited for the developer to plant 100 arbor vitaes; she wanted that screen as soon as possible. All that dust from the project would not be healthy for them, her landscaper informed her, but she told him, "I'll chance it." On the ground level, the row of trees did a fair job of blocking some of the noise and view, but from her upper windows the sight was distressing. She pulled the shades down to fight off the dust as well as the roar of the bulldozers.

Given the conditions, concentration had become almost impossible.

"You don't need the money. Why knock yourself out? The book's finished. You have plenty of columns on hand, and the bakery orders have dwindled since the construction. Take some time off. Have some fun. Get away from all this confusion." Janine advised.

"You're the one who needs to get away," said Freddie.

Both of them knew that for a long time it was Janine who actually was doing most of the writing. It had started gradually at first, with Janine making occasional suggestions about spelling or phrasing. (She was a good writer, had worked in the advertising departments of various insurance firms.) Later she began contributing ideas for anecdotes. "They don't have to be *real*," she had said. Janine had a knack of persuading Freddie to do things that she normally would not do, like pirating recipes from other sources. Naturally, Freddie often felt a sense of guilt about the situation, but then she would remember how she had once suspected Janine's mother of being a fake. Neither she nor Janine would win a medal for honesty, she mused.

Apart from her office work in the mornings, Janine had been leaving the house as much as possible. With Freddie in her present testy mood, it was a relief to escape the tensions between them. They agreed that it might be wise for both to relax for a while. While she made plans to visit friends in New York, Freddie browsed through some travel brochures. The Amish lifestyle had always intrigued her, so she signed on to a four-day trip to Lancaster County in southeastern Pennsylvania, the home to hundreds of beautiful Amish farms, operated just as they were in the 18th century.

✦ ✦ ✦ ✦ ✦ ✦

Twenty persons had signed up for the bus tour, a perfect number Freddie thought. Women, as usual, outnumbered the men, five to one, but Freddie was fortunate in having an attractive male seatmate. He was only 35, she later learned, but had prematurely gray hair, lots of it, and it was rather untidy, like the rest of his person. It was not a surprise to be told by one of the other women passengers, "He's an artist, you know. Good looking, isn't he?" Already a contest seemed to be shaping up between the unattached women. Freddie thought that the six-year age difference between them was not something to worry about at this stage.

It was a rule on the four-day trip that passengers should change seats every day, so that all could share the front places (and the available men). "That way, we all get to know each other. Part of this trip is educational, but the best part is the fun of making new friends," said the tour guide, earnestly. Junketing around, working so hard at being cheerful and efficient must be exhausting, thought Freddie, as she watched the young blonde in action.

Three nights had been booked at one centrally located hotel. Each morning the bus would set off to explore a different section of the Amish countryside. After a while, the quaintness of the costumes and the horse-drawn buggies lost their novelty, and Freddie grew weary of visiting shops and looking at painted furniture and thousands of handmade quilts, but she very much enjoyed the company of David Newcombe, who had been her seat-mate on that first day.

They were sitting next to each other on the third night, where at a genuine Amish farm a special dinner was planned as the climax of the tour.

"On the whole, I've been a little disappointed in the food so far, but these mashed potatoes must be the best in the world," she whispered. "I'm a cooking freak, you know," she said to David. "I wonder if he'll tell me his secret," she nodded towards the enormous, bearded man who was serving, and beckoned to him.

"As a professional cook, I have to tell you I've never tasted such wonderful potatoes. What sort of magic have you used?" she asked.

His craggy face smiled. At least she thought he smiled. With all those whiskers, it was hard to tell. "No special magic, ma'am. The secret of makin' 'em so smooth and creamy is a bit of cottage cheese. That, and beatin' the daylights out of them."

✶ ✶ ✶ ✶ ✶ ✶

The cottage cheese tip and David Newcombe were the strongest memories of that trip, she thought, as she and he hugged each other when they parted in Hartford.

"I got some pretty good pictures and ideas for possible paintings, but meeting you was the best part" he said, as they exchanged addresses and phone numbers.

She wondered if she would ever see David Newcombe again.

23

Charmed

"You're looking a lot perkier. Must have been a good trip," observed Janine. "Meet any one interesting? I can see you did. There's a light in your eyes that I've never seen before. What's his name?"

Freddie blushed like a teenager.

"His name is David Newcombe, originally from Boston, and now living in Hartford. He's a landscape painter."

"Too bad he isn't a landscape architect. They make more money," laughed Janine. "Well, I had a nice time, but the types I met were hardly worth talking about, mostly gays or alcoholics. Ever since the divorce I've been wary of men, I guess. Tell me about this David. Are you planning to see him again?"

For Freddie it was an effort to keep her voice calm and matter-of-fact as she described him – dark eyes, slightly high forehead, and unruly gray hair. His clothes were undistinguished and looked as if they'd been put on in a hurry, she said.

"He's definitely not Brooks Brothers, I take it?"

"Never, but he's not a slob, either," she said defensively. "As for seeing him again, who knows? It's up to him to make the first move."

"My, but we're getting a little old fashioned, aren't we? Why not give a small dinner party here, and show off your cooking? Invite four or five others. That way, you won't frighten him. Don't be coy. This is the '90's. If this man is that good, don't let him get away!"

✶ ✶ ✶ ✶ ✶ ✶

The memory of Patrick haunted her as she phoned David. This time she would play it smart, and avoid entertaining him alone. She already had acceptances from two couples – Paul Klein, an industrial designer and his lawyer wife, Audrey; and Bill Warren, a doctor, and his wife, Jennifer. They were easygoing, confident people whom David would enjoy, she hoped.

"I'm having four old friends, the Klein's and the Warren's, for dinner next Friday night at seven. They're bright, amusing couples, whom I'd love you to meet. Think you could join us? Great! You know the way to Newfield? My place, Eliot Farm, is in rather a mess right now since the fire, which I told you about, but if you can bear with the dust and the confusion, I'd love to see you."

Janine had not been mentioned. Subconsciously, she did not want Janine to meet David and had hoped that she would be in New York that evening.

When Janine heard of David's acceptance however, she said, "He's really coming? Well, I'll go to New York the next day. What are you planning for the dinner? Keep it simple, so you can relax and enjoy him. Don't try to dazzle him with some exotic dish."

"Oh, you know me better than that," laughed Freddie. "I'll go all out on the dessert, however. Wouldn't it be awful if it turned out that he was diabetic and couldn't touch sweets."

"What did you notice when you ate meals on the Amish tour?" Janine asked.

"To tell you the truth, we were having so much fun talking and laughing together that the food wasn't important," she confessed.

Entertaining was normally a pleasure, a time to try out new foods and new recipes, but she was nervous at the thought of cooking for David. By now he might have heard of her reputation as a cook and food authority, or seen some of her books in the stores, and had high expectations. But, why fret, she told herself. For superior food, all he had to do was to visit one of the many fine French restaurants in New York. He was coming to see *me*, not to taste my cooking. That thought made her even more nervous.

She was confident about the food, less confident about the looks of her house and herself. Two phone calls eased her mind: an appointment with her hairdresser, and another with Nelly, her part-time cleaning woman.

"This place is a mess. That filthy dust is over everything, but do the best you can, and make sure that the glasses on the bar are clean. I'm having a few people in for dinner tomorrow," she said.

Her effort to sound casual had not fooled Nelly. Freddie's new hair-do and a certain youthfulness in her movements betrayed her excitement. It had been a long time between men, Nelly thought, for surely a man must be the reason for Freddie's glow. "And you want everything to be just perfect. What do you plan to feed him?" she smirked.

"What makes you think it's a 'him'?" Freddie laughed. She and Nelly had known each other since high school. They were fond of each other, but sometimes Nelly could be too nosy.

"Your face and your voice, sweetie. They're a give-away. Whoever it is, he's made a new woman out of you. Do you want me to vacuum the drapes, too? I better stay an extra couple of hours. As you say, this house is a mess. There's enough dust in these drapes alone to choke a person. How about some air freshener, too?" She looked coyly at Freddie. "I'll give this job my best, just for you, old friend."

Sometimes Nelly could be a royal pain, but no one could beat her when it came to transforming a hopeless place into a "house beautiful."

Meanwhile, Freddie hunted through her recipe files.

Vichyssoise was always a safe bet, could be prepared in advance, and served hot or cold. For the main course, *Boeuf Gaston*, looked like a happy choice. One couldn't go wrong with a good, old-fashioned beef stew. A colorful, showy dessert, *Raspberry Parfait* would make a refreshing finale to the meal, she thought. This could be frozen in a fancy mold, a sure way to impress her new friend. Should salad be served? No, the soup and stew were sufficiently filling, she decided. She longed to show off her lovely French *demitasse* cups, but it would be easier to serve liqueurs instead.

Having chosen her menu, she felt more relaxed. Then she began to inspect her table silver and her linens. No problems there. One question remained: what should she wear? A full-length hostess gown would look too formal. She had good legs, why not show them, she thought, as she picked out a sleeveless, above-the-knee dress.

On the day of the party Janine helped in the den, where the large, drop leaf table, when opened, was big enough to seat eight people. She had bought some spring flowers and had made a low arrangement of modest size. "Don't over do. You mustn't show your eagerness to please," she had read somewhere. "Be casual, keep your cool," she said to Freddie as they waited for the guests' arrivals. In truth, she was almost as excited about meeting the new man as Freddie was. This David must be really special, she thought, as she watched her friend, who was anxiously double-checking the soup and the entrée.

David was the last arrival and was instantly aware that he was being inspected by the others. "Sorry to be late," he said. "I seem to have a knack for losing my way."

The truth was that he had taken his navy blazer to the cleaners and had forgotten to pick it up until the last minute. A haircut had also been neglected until a few hours before. He was not the poised, calm man whom Freddie remembered on the tour. No longer did he look the laid-back, Bohemian type. With his trim haircut, and old, but well-tailored jacket and shiny moccasins, he blended in as an average, successful young businessman.

Freddie tried – and failed – to hide her surprise as she saw him.

Amused, his eyes twinkled as he said, "Cleaned up pretty well, didn't I?"

She had to laugh as she introduced him to the others. His unexpected remark had immediately charmed them.

"When I go on those location-seeking trips I usually play the part of a starving-in-the-attic artist. I can sell more stuff to the tourists if I look a bit Bohemian. When Freddie and I met, I was trying to look like the real thing. Now you see me in my civilian life," he laughed.

"Tell us, did you sell any 'stuff,' as you call it, on your recent tour, or were you and Freddie having too much fun together?" teased Audrey Klein as she sipped her drink before dinner.

The evening was going beautifully, thought Freddie. Her first sight of David had been a shock. The scruffy, arty look was gone, but in its place a more sophisticated and witty man had evolved. He had charmed her in Amish country, but seen in her own living room, she liked him even better.

He had been traveling the United States, he said, photographing and painting the rural scenes as well as the national parks. "I paint portraits of landscapes. I don't paint portraits of people. I've tried it, and it can be a hassle. They don't, as Robbie Burns once wrote, see themselves as others see them."

Bill Warren, a Sunday painter, asked, "Have you ever thought of putting all those scenes together, a sort of 'I love America' exhibit? A friend of mine's thinking of opening a small gallery. She might be interested in your work."

"I wouldn't want to be holding my breath till that woman starts the gallery," said his wife Jennifer. After a few drinks she could show her jealous nature. "She and Bill used to go off on 'painting walks' together. At least that's what she called them."

"Now, now, let's not get catty," Bill said as he rose to leave. "Freddie, it's been a super evening. So much good food and drink, and we all enjoyed getting to know your new friend, David." He turned to him, "Seriously, I'd like to see some of your paintings. I know a lot of people in this town. Maybe we could get the ball rolling."

Later, as they stood in the kitchen loading the dishwasher, Janine said, "Don't get too excited about Bill Warren's hopeful remarks about David's paintings. He might be helpful, though. He's a popular doctor with a lot of influential friends. David's an attractive man, and he wouldn't have to go all arts and crafty to sell his work around here. Of course, nobody has *seen* his paintings – they might be drugstore art for all we know".

"But you did like him didn't you?" Freddie asked anxiously.

"Who wouldn't! Incidentally, when you described him to me, you never mentioned his wonderful, baritone voice. I can see why you fell for him."

"Who says I fell?"

"I do. But watch your step. Now that you're a partner-to-be in a shopping mall, be careful of predators with charming ways." Janine laughed as she said it, but Freddie sensed that her intent was serious.

"Don't worry, dear. I'm a grown up now. I've been scorched twice, and I don't plan to go near the fire again."

24

The Present

Janine had gone to New York the following day. What had she really thought about David? Freddie wondered. Janine had behaved in a different way with her that evening – normally she would have been affectionate, but never clingy, with her. That evening she seemed to be acting in a proprietary way towards her, as if to signal to David, "this is my property, hands off." Freddie wondered if the other guests had noticed the subtle change in Janine's behavior. Was it jealousy? Did she feel threatened by the stranger? It had always been a challenge to read what was going on in Janine's mind. Perhaps it would be wise not to try. Don't lift up that stone, unless you have the courage to see what lies under it.

It was a relief to know that she would have the house (and her thoughts) to herself for three days. Unfortunately, she also felt unusually restless and at loose ends. The party was over; where do we go from here?

Both couples had phoned that morning. Their consensus: David was charming, the food as good as ever, and they'd seldom had "a more congenial evening."

There was no word from David.

For two days she wandered about the house, elated one minute, dejected the next. It was as if she had been on a sugar 'high' then crashed. She was reading half-heartedly through a catalog of kitchen tools when she heard the front doorbell.

David was standing at the door, a clumsily wrapped package in one hand. "I meant to call you and tell you what a great time I had, but I was too busy working on this," he said, grinning. "Go ahead, open it."

In her pleasure and astonishment, Freddie almost dropped the brown paper package. David anxiously watched her expression as she tore apart the wrappings.

"My God! David, this is wonderful. For years I've wanted a painting of this old house."

On impulse, she ran to him and kissed him full on the mouth. It surprised and pleased them both. They looked at each other and laughed.

"I guess that means you liked it."

"Like it? It's the most perfect present you could have given me. How did you manage to do it, in such short time?"

He explained how he had come around the next morning with his camera and taken several shots of the house from various angles. ("I had to work fast to avoid being seen.") Actually, he admitted, the painting was easy, had taken less time than the chore of having it framed. The trick with watercolors, he said, is to work swiftly. With oils, you can paint over your mistakes, with water colors, you have to get it right the first time."

"And did you?"

"Want to know the truth? It took me at least five tries to capture the spirit of this old place. Except for barns and silos, I'd never made a watercolor of a house."

"Well, you can give yourself four gold stars for this one. Oh, David, you'll never guess how much this means to me."

"I think I've guessed," he said, as he tilted up her chin and kissed her.

25

A Business Arrangement

In the days that followed Freddie felt light-headed and silly, much as she had felt many years ago when she first met George. Fortunately, she was doing very little writing. Concentration was impossible. She passed the time dusting and re-dusting the furniture, looking at trashy shows on TV, chatting inanely with friends on the phone, and denying to Janine that she was in love with David.

"Don't try to fool me. You're hooked. I guess that painting of the house tipped the scale in his favor. I really like it. That spot over the mantle is perfect for it. When are you going to see him again? Has he lured you up to his place to look at his 'etchings' – I mean *paintings?*" Janine teased.

"I haven't seen him since he gave me the watercolor, but we're having lunch in three days, then he'll show me his whole collection," Freddie said.

"And that ain't all!" laughed Janine.

Janine's humor did not always mesh with Freddie's moods, and this was one of those times. She felt very much attracted to David, but did not want to rush into something she might regret. After all, he was a virtual stranger. There were still too many unknowns in his history. Why, at 35, was he still single? What about his family in Boston?

And what about their age difference?

In three days she might know more. Meanwhile she did some window-shopping for a new wardrobe.

✶ ✶ ✶ ✶ ✶ ✶

Thursday had never been a lucky day in Freddie's life. Her father, Gretchen and Al had died on Thursdays. Normally, she would have avoided making dates on a Thursday, but when David proposed it, she could not say, "Sorry, but I have a thing about Thursdays. Can't we make it another day?"

So on Thursday, at noon, she was sitting tensely in the living room when she saw his station wagon arrive. It was not a new car, and it had a lived-in look, an aristocratic shabbiness. In its day, ten years ago, the big Buick would have been labeled "top of the line."

She ran out the door to meet him, even before he had climbed out of his car, and slid onto the seat beside him.

No kiss this time.

"Where do you want to go?" he asked, smiling. In Hartford we can offer you French, Indonesian, Japanese, Chinese, or plain old Italian."

She laughed, "What a pity. I just had a yen for some roast Yak from Tibet. If no Tibetan food, how about Chinese?"

"What a tactful choice. You must have been looking into my wallet lately," he said as they drove off.

The Hunan Wok was more elaborate than most Chinese restaurants. In the entrance stood a traditional fixture in those places, a large tank filled with exotic fish, on hand to divert the carryout customers as they waited. Within, the large trayceilinged dining room was a surprise, with its enormous panels of misty Chinese landscapes that ranged around the walls.

"I can see why you like this place," Freddie said, as they ordered Won Ton soup for two.

Bit by bit, as they talked, they peeled away some of the unknowns about themselves. Art was not David's first choice of career, he admitted. The youngest of three sons, he had always planned to follow his brothers into the family's banking business. For generations the Newcombes had been fixtures in Boston's financial and social circles. Then, at Harvard, David had taken a gut course in Art Appreciation, and to his family's horror, decided to switch to a Fine Arts major.

In his family's narrow view, he said, "Art was for sissies, or even worse, gays. Here I was, throwing away a solid life of comfort and security to become a certain failure, a pathetic creature in a smock and beret."

To make matters more shocking for them, he had fallen in love with a girl from *Hartford*, of all second-rate places. She wasn't even a Radcliffe girl, but he followed her to her hometown, with marriage in view. Needless to say, his family gave him no support, financial or moral.

"Then what happened?"

"We lived in a tiny apartment for two years. Margaret, that was her name, supported us, while I desperately tried to get a job as a commercial artist. We never did get married. I think she just lost faith in me, and I couldn't blame her. She's married now, with three kids."

Eventually his family could no longer bear to ignore what they considered his sordid life and set up a small trust fund for him. "For the past few years I've been surviving on that," he said.

"Actually, I make a pretty good living on these scenic trips. On an hourly basis, I figure I can earn about $160 an hour or $640 for an afternoon's work. Not bad, is it?"

Freddie was astonished, and pleased, too.

He continued, "First I visit the scene, get a feeling of its character, then take several pictures. When I get home – or in some cases, to my hotel room – I practice doing my landscapes. Once I get them right, the painting goes very fast. I can turn out a $30 painting, mat and all, in about 15 minutes. Come and get it folks, a real painting."

"You sound a bit discontented, however. Have you ever thought of switching to oils?" she asked.

"Many times. There's far more money in that field. But, in every respect, it costs more money. Your materials are expensive and you'd need some kind of space, a small studio, at least."

As she listened, Freddie's imagination was working at top speed. Already she was picturing herself as David's fairy godmother. She had more money now, far more than she needed. She smiled as she cracked open her fortune cookie. *"Fortune smiles on you today. Make the most of it."*

✶ ✶ ✶ ✶ ✶ ✶

As they left the restaurant and drove to David's apartment, Freddie sat close to David, but not too close. Her urge to sit nearer to him, their hips touching, was tamed. This time, she told herself, she would control her emotions. The visit to his apartment might lead to a more serious involvement than she was prepared to make. Concentrate on the art; pretend that his paintings were her major concern. Which was nonsense, she knew. His apartment, in a three-story stucco building, in an undistinguished part of town, was as uninspired as she had imagined. Ah, but the walls, they were astonishing – almost every inch of the small living room was hung with simply-framed landscapes, scores of them. Slowly walking around the room, Freddie tried to disguise her amazement. As if in a formal exhibit, each painting had a printed description next to it: *The Voodoos, Bryce Canyon, Utah; Nevada Falls, Glacier Point, Yosemite, California; The Grand Tetons, Wyoming; South Rim, the Grand Canyon, Arizona.*

"America really has such extraordinary scenery," she finally said. The impact of his paintings had left her speechless.

David had been carefully watching her expression as she wandered, bemused, in his apartment. There were paintings everywhere, even in the bathroom.

"David, what you've accomplished is amazing. I'm no expert, but I can't help feeling you should lift this entire collection and move it where it would get a really wide showing. I'd like to help you. Would you let me? Now don't get too sensitive or proud. Call it a business arrangement between us. I could be your agent, say. What do you think?"

They were standing several feet apart. Neither made a move towards the other. He sat down into a well-worn wing chair, and ran his hand through his thick hair, dazed by her suggestion.

"Frankly, dear, your idea stuns me. Give me time to think this through."

In answer, Freddie walked around to the side of his chair and put a hand on his shoulder.

"Darling, I don't want to push you into anything. I like you very, very much, and I want to be a part of your success. I know how suffocating it can be to be dominated by someone, so I promise I'll keep out of your way."

For the next hour they excitedly discussed David's career possibilities. Freddie need not have worried about fending off any romantic overtures. It was so exhilarating to contemplate their future partnership together.

26

The Steam Engine

A few days later Donald Bailey had a lunch date with Freddie in town. For some reason, she had not wanted to meet him in his office. Doesn't want to hear my meter ticking, he thought. Even in a small town, top lawyers could charge $175 an hour. Her voice on the phone had sounded strangely different, like his daughter's had when she told him he was going to be a grandfather. Through his friend, Bill Warren, he had heard of Freddie's new – what should he be called – beau? That was too old fashioned a name. Just call him an "interest," for according to Bill, Freddie was surely interested in this new man, David Newcombe.

"An artist, you say? And you've seen his work? Obviously, it must have impressed you, or you wouldn't be sitting with me, all excited about going into business with him." Bailey smiled at her. He had never seen her so elated.

"Who else, besides you, has seen his work? Wouldn't it be a smart move to have a pro look over his collection? An impartial judge? Let's be honest, Freddie, your interest isn't exactly objective. I hear he's very attractive."

Freddie blushed. "Don't be a tease, Donald. I guess I just want you to give your approval before I jump off the cliff."

He laughed. "But you'll jump off anyway, won't you?" His clients frequently asked his advice and promptly ignored it. "Before you make any plans, give me a day or two to think this over."

It was Freddie's turn to laugh. "Why, that's what David said! It seems as if everybody's trying to stop me from doing something foolish. As you and I both know, I have more money now. More than I need, and once the mall gets going, I'll have even more. I won't go hog wild, I promise you."

Bailey took another sip of his coffee. "Have you talked this over with Janine?"

She hesitated before answering. Should she tell him that there had been a coolness between them ever since the sale of the land? He had never really trusted Janine, she knew. "No, we haven't discussed it. She seemed to like David when she met him, but she feels wary about him. Frankly, I suspect she's a little jealous about a newcomer taking my attention."

More than attention, the lawyer thought. However, Freddie's idea of acting as an agent for this artist might work out. On the other hand, she might go overboard and finance a gallery for him, or even *build* one. A wealthy woman in love could be unpredictable.

When he returned to his office Bailey phoned Dick Lester in Hartford. Lester, a former police officer turned investigator, was a useful man to know. "Dick, Bailey here. I have a small job for you, nothing interesting. One of my clients wants to go into business with some artist, whom she recently met. I'm trying to stop her from doing anything crazy. The man's name is Newcombe, David Newcombe, from Hartford. Originally from Boston, where I'm told his family's prominent in banking. I'd appreciate it if you'd run a routine check on him." They chatted about other matters for a few more minutes, then Bailey said, "Remember that fire on the Eliot land? They suspected arson, but nothing came of it. Maybe they should have called you in on the case." In Bailey's mind there was no question that it was arson, but who would have set the fire, and why? Could Jim Bankson have had a hand in it? Bankson had tried for years to talk Freddie into selling those acres, and there was chat around real estate circles that Bankson was livid when he heard that he'd been bested in the deal. He and Janine were still seen having their coffee breaks at the diner. There was something uneasy-making about *her*, too. Freddie was still loyal to her, but he sensed that she was beginning to loosen herself from Janine's dominance. And about time, he thought.

★ ★ ★ ★ ★ ★

Dick Lester reported to Bailey three days later. David Newcombe was lily pure on all counts: respected in the neighborhood, paid his bills on time, gave modestly to local charities, was quiet and thoughtful to his fellow tenants, had no serious girl (or boy) friends, smoked and drank in moderation, and had nothing on the police blotter, not even a parking ticket. To top it all, his family, prominent Bostonians, had set up a small trust fund for him.

"I'd give him a four-star rating, any day," he said.

Bailey was perplexed. Should he confess to Freddie that he'd run a check on her friend David? I think not, he decided, as he picked up the phone to call her. "I've given a lot of thought to your idea of going into business with David Newcombe, and it doesn't seem like such a bad investment."

"Checked up on him, didn't you?" Freddie laughed. "I know how you operate, Donald. Caution, caution. And I'm happy to feel that I have a protector. You're like a father to me, and I'm grateful. It won't surprise you to learn that ever since our conversation I've set the wheels in motion."

"What do you mean? What have you been doing? I've got to hand it to you, Freddie, you move fast."

"I feel I have to. There's something so unreal about this whole situation, so unexpected, that I fear the idea might evaporate, like a dream. David doesn't even know what I've done. In fact I haven't heard a word from him."

"Maybe he's cautious, too, like me."

"That's it. He's talented, but he's not a pusher."

"And you want to be the steam engine." Bailey smiled into the phone.

In an extraordinary burst of energy, Freddie had been working nonstop towards her goal. A visit to her editor, Blake Jennings, of the *Newfield Bee*, gained for her the name of an art critic in Hartford. "I'm interested in buying some paintings, purely as an investment, and I'd like to have his opinion," she said.

"You'll get it, but it might cost you." He replied. "Incidentally, what about your own work? Our contract's about due to run out. Do you want to continue, or do you want to quit, now that you're going to be a very wealthy woman?"

Freddie laughed. "I've been meaning to talk to you about the column. Frankly, I'm growing a bit tired of the job. The clichés don't roll out the way they used to, and the royalties from the two cookbooks are helpful, but I think I've become weary of writing, in general."

"So you're going into the art business? Ever think of starting an art gallery? This town could use one."

"Blake, you've read my mind. I'll let you know if it happens," she said as she left the office. Perhaps she had said too much. Re-entering his office she said, "Please don't say anything to anyone, particularly Rosie, about this." Rose Winfred, the society columnist was known as "Nosy Rosie."

Country Realty was only three blocks away, so she called on Leslie Jenks. "This isn't a big deal, Leslie, and it simply might waste your time, but can you think of a modest space that could be used for an art gallery? I have an artist friend who might be looking for a place. He'll be in touch with you. Meanwhile, please keep this confidential."

As she walked with Freddie to the door, Leslie wondered who the 'he' might be.

27

Criticism

Martin Reuben was a freelance art critic. His art columns appeared occasionally, and while they had been praised for their lucidity and art knowledge, they didn't pay the rent. His illustrations for children's books were also praised, but he was usually short of cash, and would welcome any odd jobs that were offered. Freddie's phone call lifted his spirits.

"Yes, I think I could find the time to critique your friend's work. I usually charge a fee of $500. I give it more than a quick look, you see. You can count on me to give an honest judgment, whether it's good and deserves promotion, or whether it's trash and should be dumped. Good or bad, I'll ask for my fee up front."

He was surprised that Freddie accepted his terms so easily. He had never asked for so high a fee, but something about the woman's voice, her eagerness, gave him the courage. They agreed to meet at the Newcombe apartment the following day.

As they met in front of the building, Freddie handed him $500 in cash. She was not impressed by Reuben's appearance: short with greasy black hair, carefully combed over a bald spot. Oh, well, it was his knowledge that counted. David was nervously waiting as they came into his living room. Reuben did not hide his astonishment at the size and scope of the collection.

"My God, this is incredible. How long did it take you to paint all of these?"

With just one look, he could tell that this man was a real artist, but Reuben had been paid a large fee to give his valued opinion, so he had to be unhurried and serious. Take your time, he told himself. David and Freddie anxiously watched him as he walked very slowly around the room. Reuben's face was expressionless, as a judge's should be. He was silent. All of them were. The tension was too much for Freddie, who whispered, "How about the two of us sitting in the kitchen with a cup of coffee?"

For almost an hour they sat silently in the kitchen. Finally Reuben came in and joined them. "I think you have something here," he said, "but there's a catch. They're watercolors. Put the same kind of skill in oils, that wonderful sense of color and place, and there's no telling how far you could go. Even Winslow Homer switched from watercolors to oils. If you want to go for serious money, take a course in oil painting."

Freddie never told David that she had paid a fee for Reuben's judgment. She simply said that she had asked him, through a mutual friend, to give an opinion about a friend's work. It would have upset him to know about that $500 fee, but Reuben's expertise was worth it. He had suggested re-creating the same scenes, but in oil instead. It was simply a matter of learning to paint in another medium. Oils were considered far easier to master, so it shouldn't be too difficult to make the changeover, he advised. And David agreed, though there was one problem – money.

✶ ✶ ✶ ✶ ✶ ✶

Another conference with Bailey was to be held the next week. Meanwhile, Freddie had paid a second visit to Leslie Jenks in her real estate office. As she explained, "The situation has changed since we last spoke about my artist friend. It may be some time before he's ready to give a full-fledged exhibit, but let me know if you spot a place that might be worth considering. And remember, keep this confidential." It was important to be mum about her plans. Not even Janine must know.

When Freddie walked into his office, Bailey noticed a different aura around her – she seemed more business-like, less bewitched. Which, in truth, she was. There had been no romantic interlude after Reuben's departure, not even any temptation. Both were too keyed up, their minds too excited about the possibilities ahead.

"Believe it or not, Donald, I've done something very sensible, and what's more, I followed your advice about calling in a pro. For a fee, I got an art critic, Martin Reuben, to give an opinion about David's work."

"And?"

"And he feels that David has real talent. The man seemed to be genuinely impressed, but believes that to be really successful, David should switch to another medium. Change from watercolors to oils."

"Would you call that a 'rave review'?" Bailey asked.

"I call it common sense. The real problem, of course, is money. David, as you probably know, has a trust fund, but not enough money to pay for all the extras that such a change would mean."

Bailey had been prepared for Freddie's proposal: a loan to David until he had completed the changeover and was ready to mount an exhibit of his new work. When a suitable gallery had been found, Freddie would act as his agent. Reuben, she said, had been very helpful in suggesting a good teacher, and had given him a rough idea of the materials he should buy. Freddie confessed that she had already visited Bailey's realtor friend, Leslie.

"Don't rush out and buy a building, Freddie. Let's move in baby steps. One important thing has now been determined, that David has a real chance of being successful, as successful as one can be in an 'iffy' business. When am I going to meet your talented friend? Let's set up a date right now. Does next Thursday suit you?"

"Quickly, she replied, "Sorry, Thursday won't do. How about Tuesday? That's always been my lucky day."

28

Proper Bostonians

David and Bailey sized each other up when they met on Tuesday. The lawyer had a homely, genial face, which David immediately trusted. To Bailey, David's premature gray hair was a surprise and he was unprepared for the mellowness of the voice, which made him seem older than his 35 years. Each liked the looks of the other. David had carefully made notes for the meeting. He had also brought with him some color photos of some of his current paintings. "My bona fides," he said, smiling, as Bailey quickly scanned them.

"Freddie's already told me all about Mr. Reuben's opinions about your work. There's no problem about your talent. Have you any figures about the cost involved in changing to another medium?"

David was delighted to show that he had done his homework. Donald Bailey was no accountant, but he was pleased to see the meticulous details of David's report. This man was no dummy, he mused. Within two hours a tentative plan for a partnership was formed, and Freddie gave David a check to cover the first costs.

They kissed as they went their separate ways. It had been a happy day for them both. When he reached his apartment David immediately called his mother in Boston. Emily Slocum Newcombe had long believed in her son's talent, but was disappointed that he had not lived the comfortable, high achieving life of his brothers. Several of his framed paintings were hung on the walls of her guest rooms. They were not quite "important enough" to merit space in the living room, she judged. When she heard the news of her son's new, apparently rich, friend and partner, she was surprised and pleased.

"We'd love to meet him. Perhaps you could both drive up here for a weekend?" (A wealthy sponsor might solve a lot of problems.)

"Sure, Mom. But, I have to tell you it's a *she*, not a he."

His mother tried to sound casual. "That makes it all the more interesting. What's her name? Is it anyone we know?" (Of course not, David always had such odd taste in women.) Luckily, she didn't ask where she met him. (On a bus trip? How extraordinary!) Or how long he'd known her. He left her with the following details to absorb: Fredrika Eliot, known as Freddie, was born 41 years ago in Newfield, Connecticut; well known as a talented cook and cookbook writer; descendant of prosperous tobacco growers in the Connecticut River valley; part owner of a new shopping mall; never married; lives with a personal assistant, Janine Fulton. There were certain elements that worried her. At 41, Fredrika was older than David and almost past the childbearing age. Why had she never married? And who was this Fulton woman who shared the house with her? And where was Newfield? She could barely find it on the map. Oh, well, not all of us are lucky enough to be born in Boston, she sighed.

✶ ✶ ✶ ✶ ✶ ✶

Freddie's seed money had unusually fast results. With his new painting equipment, David signed up for private lessons in oil technique. In a surprisingly short time, he learned to transform his watercolor landscapes into excellent, commercially promising paintings. Martin Reuben came again (without a fee) and was really enthusiastic about David's progress. "At this rate, you'll be ready to exhibit in a few more weeks. Didn't I tell you oil painting was far easier to master? Keep it up, and I'll be writing a column about you someday."

During a recent visit to David's, Freddie immediately noticed that the look of his living room walls had radically changed, as the subtle colorings of his former works were traded for far larger pieces with more dramatic tones. It was time for a serious search for a combined studio and gallery. They looked around in the Hartford area, and found the rental prices discouraging. Freddie hesitated before suggesting Newfield.

"The other day I was shown a small house in Newfield. It's in a good section of town, has an interesting history as the home of a former sculptor, but it 'needs work,' as they say in the ads. It's like mine, a late Victorian, with high ceilings, which would be fine in a gallery. Shall we drive over and check it out?" she asked.

Compared with the Hartford prices, the Langford House (named for the late sculptor) was a give-away, Freddie thought. Unfortunately, it was not a rental. However, as Leslie Jenks explained, it could be bought for "almost nothing," just the payment of the back taxes owed to the town. Jenks, naturally, showed them other properties, but they kept returning to the Langford House. The ever-cautious Bailey had gone with them on a second tour of the house. He was wary of Freddie's increasing emotional and financial involvement with David and was not too keen on a further entanglement, but he finally conceded that the old house might be a good investment. He had been taken to see David's new paintings and had been impressed, and had even tried to purchase one of them. "You really deserve to have a place where you can show your work," he'd said.

David had taken some pictures of the Langford house, which he showed to his family when he and Freddie arrived in Boston a month later. The house sale had gone off without problems, though they were still jockeying for prices on the renovation. The Newcombe house on Beacon Hill and David's parents, Henry and Emily, were exactly as Freddie had imagined: dignified, conservative, and predictable. As gray-haired as his son, Henry Newcombe had his son's self-mocking charm, but one sensed an enormous confidence that generations of power and wealth could bring. He peered through horn-rimmed glasses at the picture of the house with the same intense interest that he had given to Freddie when they met. "You say this house belonged to some well known sculptor, James Langford? Never heard of him."

David laughed. "You wouldn't, Dad. Sculpture's not your thing. It's not a big place, as you can see, but Freddie and I feel that it would be perfect as a combined studio and gallery."

At the words "Freddie and I" Emily Newcombe inwardly flinched. A short woman, her brown hair, worn in an old fashioned bun, gave her a prim, schoolmarm look. Her first impression of Freddie had been good: her open, natural look made her seem much younger than her 41 years; her casually expensive clothes and her poise, she found attractive. She was not "Boston" but she was not "small town," either. After two days, however, there was something about the woman that Emily found disturbing. Why would an attractive, obviously wealthy, intelligent woman become so deeply involved with David, a younger, more naïve, man? She sensed a bossiness there, a need to dominate. Most disturbing of all, why would this woman, who must have had the pick of the town's most suitable men, be living with another woman? Years ago, when two mature women lived together, they called it a "Boston marriage."

29

Room at the Inn

As they drove home after the Newcombes' traditional Sunday lunch of roast beef, neither of them said much. "How do you think it went?" David asked at last. "They seemed to like you very much."

Faint praise, thought Freddie. She could still feel Emily's eyes sizing her up. Bostonians, she thought, were always snobs about outsiders, and Emily Newcombe was no different. She had seemed relieved, however, that her son had found a backer who was not only socially presentable, but appeared to be financially solvent. "I hope so!" was her response.

David had insisted on using his old car for the drive to Boston. It had been driven without incident for more than 100,000 miles and seemed fit enough for another long run, when suddenly the right front tire went flat. David was disgusted. In all the years he'd owned the car, he'd never had a tire problem. They had decided to return home by way of one of David's favorite scenic routes. It was a very pretty drive, but far away from a gas station, or even a house. For a few crestfallen minutes they waited on a grassy edge of the road and hopefully prayed for a passing car to rescue them. Two cars went by without stopping. Then two more rushed past. The two of them might as well have been holding up a sign saying, "Lepers."

David was becoming more and more agitated and mortified. "Honestly, I feel like such an ass. Would you believe I've never changed a tire before?"

Freddie itched to tell him that, years ago, her father had taught her how to jack up a car and change a tire. He had also taught her how to drive a tractor and a snowplow, but for the time being, it seemed best to hide those "masculine" accomplishments. The sky began to darken. David became almost petulant in his frustration.

"Damn it. I shouldn't have been so cheap about buying new tires. I don't suppose you'd know anything about changing a flat? You 'new' women can do about anything these days."

Freddie laughed. "So glad you asked me. Yes, I have fixed a flat or two. Let's check your trunk for a jack."

It was becoming increasingly dark and light rain was falling as David held a flashlight while Freddie worked on the tire. She had one knee on the grass and was aware of her natural awkwardness as she fumbled with the tools. It had been at least ten years since she had been in this situation, and she was younger then, and in better shape. She tried not to grunt. David was silent, and grateful that at least he was helpful in lifting the damaged tire and replacing it with the spare.

"It's too late now to look for a garage and try to get it fixed," he said. "I just remembered there was a nice little inn not far from here, *Wagon Wheels*, where we could get a light meal and clean up. Maybe they could put us up for the night. What do you think?"

Freddie was not keen on returning home in her dirty, disheveled condition: there was a large hole in her hose, her good tweed skirt was grass stained; her hands and one cheek had streaks of oil; and her hair had turned kinky from the rain. A shower and a clean, *single* bed seemed inviting.

"I'll stay in the car while you run in and see if there's a vacancy," she suggested.

The inn's owner, Oliver Mason, had been expecting David, who had phoned him from Boston the day before. "I figured you'd be here earlier. Are you all right?" he asked.

"I'm O.K., but my friend's not too well. I think we'll need two singles. Cancel the double. Are you still serving those wonderful steaks? We've had a car problem and we need a pick-me-up."

Mason tried to mask his surprise when Freddie entered and signed in. Whatever the "car problem" was, it was she who had worked on it. David looked tired and harassed, but Freddie looked beaten. All she wanted to do was to have a good meal, undress, stand under a warm shower and climb into bed – alone.

30

Second Thoughts

"The romance seems to be heating up," Janine said to Jim Bankson at the diner the next morning. "They spent the night at some inn in Rhode Island. Car trouble, she said. I thought David Newcombe had more imagination than that. Apparently, Freddie was being inspected by David's stuffy parents. No doubt they're wondering what sort of a fairy godmother had entered their baby boy's life."

"Do I detect a little jealousy here, Janine? Are you concerned about all the money she's been spending on this so-called partnership? Have you seen that old, rundown house that they plan to make into a gallery? I wouldn't want it as a gift. Put a match to it, and pfft!"

Janine was indeed concerned. Day by day, she sensed that she was losing control of Freddie. No longer was she a confidante. Freddie talked a lot with her lawyer, but seldom shared her thoughts with anyone else. Except David, whom she saw or spoke with every day. She had gone with Freddie to look at David's growing collection of oils and had been astonished. No wonder Freddie had been so eager to promote him.

She seldom saw David, though once a week he was likely to stay for dinner at the house with them. He was always good company, yet she felt a certain lack of frankness in his manner with her, as if he were measuring her in the same way that she was studying him. Freddie noticed this, and one day as they sat in the office, she challenged her. They had been checking Freddie's bank statements, a chore which Janine had usually done.

Taking off her glasses, she looked at Janine, through half closed eyes. "You really don't care much for him, do you?"

Abashed, Janine finally replied, "Of course I do. David's a very attractive, talented man, but I do worry about your growing involvement with him. Next thing I know, you'll be telling me you're going to marry him."

Freddie blushed and laughed nervously. "It could happen, but the idea would have to come from him. Remember, Janine, I'm an old fashioned girl."

Janine was not convinced. Freddie was obviously crazy about the man. It was just a matter of time before Freddie married him, and Janine would be out of a job – and a home.

✶ ✶ ✶ ✶ ✶ ✶

Several weeks went by. Freddie was spending most of her time with contractors, house painters and electricians. David's time in the old house had slackened off. He was not good at dickering about costs, he said. "I trust you to deal with these people. It's more important for me to work on my technique. Reuben thinks I need a few more lessons, and he's rented me some space in his studio."

"Darling, I understand, but I'll miss you." She'd said. What could she say? Admit to David how needy she was? Fortunately, she was so preoccupied with the plans for the gallery that days passed before she realized that David was no longer present. They had talked often on the phone but she'd noticed a different timbre in his voice, a hesitance, which alarmed her. She called him but he seldom called her. Could it be that he wanted to back out of their agreement? The very thought made her sweat.

They agreed to meet for lunch in Hartford. It was not on a Thursday, but it was equally unlucky. With painful hesitation, David broke the news to her.

"You're a wonderful person, Freddie, and it hurts me so to tell you, but I don't think our arrangement's going to work. I'll always admire you, but my feelings for you have changed. There was a time when I even thought of marriage, but that's gone, too. I think we ought to cut our losses."

Freddie sat speechless at the table, then quickly left before he could see her weeping.

31

Oreo

Later that evening, Benjamin Little, owner of Little's Pet Store, told his wife, "The weirdest thing happened today. Around lunchtime, things were slow and I was reading my paper when the door chime rings and this tall, well-dressed woman comes into the store. She was blowing her nose and her eyes were red, and at first I thought she had a bad cold, but then I realized she was crying. I made her sit on a chair till she calmed down. She'd been passing by and had fallen in love with the little black-and-white kitten in the window, she said. You know, the one you like. The one that's all black, but with white paws, face, ears and tip of the tail. Within minutes, we'd made a deal, and off we went with a carrier, litter box, cat food, litter and the kitten. A lot to carry, believe me, and to make it tougher, I had to help her find her car. She was so upset she couldn't remember where she'd parked it. She was hugging that kitten so hard I was scared she'd squeeze it to death. Poor woman, I hope she made it back home safely."

✶ ✶ ✶ ✶ ✶ ✶

Janine attempted to hide her surprise when Freddie finally arrived home. She had been driving aimlessly for hours, with the kitten in his carrier on the seat beside her. She did not explain why she had – on impulse – suddenly acquired a pet, or what had happened between her and David, and Janine was smart enough not to ask. Two days later she heard the story. It was one of the saddest days of her life, Freddie admitted.

"I was so caught up in all the details about the house that I failed to notice that we had begun to change towards each other. Perhaps we rushed into things too soon. But, at the time, it seemed so right. His painting was going so well, and the house plans were progressing. Tell me, Janine, what happened, what did I do wrong?" she wailed.

"Nothing, dear. Stop beating up on yourself. Have you talked to Donald Bailey about this?"

Freddie explained that she had talked with Bailey the day before, and that he had been "very tactful. Never scolded me for becoming involved with a man I hardly knew. From the business point of view, he said, I might actually come out on top, apart from the $800 loan I'd made to David. The real estate market was rising fast, he told me, and when that little house was restored, I could make a 'nice piece of change' on the deal."

Nevertheless, Freddie was heartsick. Thank God for the little kitten, thought Janine as she watched Freddie playing with "Oreo," as she had named him. "When do you think he'll be old enough to sleep on my bed?" Freddie asked, as she held the kitten next to her cheek. At night he had been sleeping in his carrier, next to her bed, but during the day Freddie carried him with her constantly. Freddie desperately needed someone to love.

32

Architecture

Rosie Winfred, the woman's page editor on the *Newfield Bee*, had not acted on the rumor about Freddie's plans for the gallery, and Freddie was much relieved. Publicity was the last thing she needed. With Bailey's approval she had decided to continue with her plans for the renovation of the Langford house. "As the building would not be used as a gallery," she told her architect, Neil Walsh, when they met a week later at the site, "we won't have to worry anymore about a sophisticated lighting scheme."

Walsh was intrigued by her use of the word "we." Through the grapevine, he had already heard rumors that the partnership between Eliot and Newcombe had collapsed. The artist had seemed the more passive of the pair, less intense about his likes and dislikes. Fredrika was extremely attractive, he thought, but her personality was at times commanding. There was no question, however, about her love and pride in the man. You could see it in her eyes. And now those eyes looked dull, the spark had gone.

It would have been fun to design some creative lighting effects, he thought, but working with Fredrika Eliot was stimulating in itself, and he looked forward to completing the job with her.

"What, then, are we aiming for? A conventional sort of place that would be an easy rental? Or something more dramatic?" he asked, smiling.

Freddie's reply was, as he had hoped, "Oh, let's go for the dramatic. I think I'm ready for a real change." What kind of change, she wondered, as she noticed for the first time that Neil Walsh had very kindly eyes.

✶ ✶ ✶ ✶ ✶ ✶

Removing David's painting from its honored spot in the middle of the fireplace wall was less painful that Freddie had feared, but she could not bring herself to destroy it. Janine offered to take it up to the attic. "Now it's in the right place, with all the other ghosts of the past."

Oreo, a month after his purchase, had grown enormously, but was still full of kittenish charm, and was now large enough to sleep on Freddie's bed, which calmed and comforted her. "Who would have thought that a kitten, impulsively bought at a desperate time, would bring me such peace?" she said to Janine, as she sat on the living room couch slowly stroking Oreo. "Is this what they mean by 'pet therapy' in the nursing homes? Believe me, it really works! I now have the courage and the stamina to fight with the carpenters and painters every day."

Janine laughed. "How about your new friend, Neil? From what you report, you and he get along *wonderfully*."

"Stop that insinuating tone, Janine. I like Neil Walsh as a friend and architect, and like Oreo, he's been a comfort to me, but I don't have to stroke his fur, thank God!"

Nor did she have to stroke his ego. One of the most attractive of Neil's traits was his serenity, which had been so useful in times of strife with the carpenters and electricians on a job. When she arrived on the scene Neil was trying to explain – very tactfully – to Tom, the head carpenter, why he wanted him to use one wall of the former studio as an area of built-in shelves and closets. And he had added another feature, which the carpenter had called ridiculous.

Neil said, "Freddie, you may agree with Tom that the idea of building a sleeping loft is crazy, I know, but with these extra high ceilings, there's a lot of wasted space, so it'll be very handy to have more sleeping space down here."

Grudgingly, the carpenter, a slightly stooped, gray-haired man, nodded and went upstairs to continue his work. He was pleased with the architect's idea of building cornices over the living room windows, but remained cool about some of the other plans. Originally, the space of one of the three bedrooms upstairs had been given over to a very large, old-fashioned bathroom. This, according to Neil's plan, would now be split into two compact, but very modern units. A third bathroom would somehow be carved out of the living room area. Well, that's *his* problem, the carpenter thought, as he began his measurements.

"Tom's not entirely sold on me or my ideas, but we've worked together before. He's more of the old school, but he's a great craftsman, though I have to handle him with kid gloves. I'm told that, at home, he still has his grandfather's pedal driven tools," said Neil as he offered a sandwich to Freddie. Two or three days a week, while he was on the job, Neil brought enough coffee and sandwiches for them both.

Looking at Neil as she sipped her coffee, Freddie knew that she found him more and more likable. He was not handsome, at 45, with thinning hair and the start of a small paunch, and he was an inch or two shorter than she, but his smile was a winner. Widowed, like her father at an early age, he had (with his mother's help) raised a successful son, now in college. Neil drew a snapshot out of his wallet and passed it to her. "Neil, Jr., a fine arts major at Yale. He may go to architecture school.

Right now it's too early to tell. I don't see as much of him as I'd like. It's tough to compete with a pretty girl," he smiled as he put the picture back into his wallet.

"You have a Neil, Jr. My poor father tried so hard to have an Alfred, III, but he finally had to settle for an Alberta and a Fredrika," she laughed.

Neil was silent. He knew the story of the Eliot sisters. Her father's history of bad luck was also familiar. Fredrika's romantic past was a mystery, however, and Neil was too tactful to probe. He had heard recently that David was under the influence of Martin Reuben, the critic and artist. Reuben was claiming himself as the discoverer of a "major new talent." So be it, thought Neil. To him, David seemed the kind who would always need a prop through life. Freddie was lucky to be rid of him. That's what her friend, Janine, had said to him when they met recently at a party. Who was this Janine? he wondered. Though not much older than Freddie, the woman had a strange dominance over her. There was something about Janine, attractive though she was, that Neil didn't trust. Was it the slightly oriental set of her eyes and prominent cheekbones or her over-friendly manner, which made him wary of her? It would be so healthful for Freddie to get out from under Janine's influence. She needed to have another interest, besides her current preoccupation with the house. She had told him "I'm clumsy, like my father. Always the last person in school to be picked for a team." So sports were out. Perhaps she might enjoy flying? He had bought a small plane some years ago and spent some of the best hours of his life at the controls of his Piper Cub.

33

The Wild Blue Yonder

One day, after some rewarding time working out details on the house, Neil asked her, "Freddie, I'd like to open up a whole new world for you. You told me yourself that you needed a change. How would you feel about taking a flying lesson in my old Piper Cub? Are you ready for a challenge?"

In a rare moment of recklessness, Freddie had answered, "Why not!"

✶ ✶ ✶ ✶ ✶ ✶

Flying had never been a good experience for Freddie, and whenever possible, she had chosen to travel by ship or train. It was not fear of dying but the feeling of claustrophobia that bothered her. She didn't like the noise, either nor the bodies of total strangers pressed against her. And she hated the food, as any fine cook would. To top it all, airlines were notorious for losing luggage. Arrive in London, and your bags end up in Vienna.

There were a hundred reasons to say "no" to Neil's suggestion, but it must have been the same impulsiveness that made her buy the kitten that led her to say "yes." Sitting next to him as they drove the ten miles to the small, private airfield, she had the same feeling of excitement and anticipation that she'd felt when she and her sister and father boarded the old Queen Mary on their first trip to England.

Neil introduced her to Bob Curcio, the young manager of the airfield. "My friend, Freddie, is used to the jumbos, and hates them. I'm going to show her the thrill of flying in a human-sized plane. Is mine all fueled and ready to go?"

"Sure thing, Neil. We love to show newcomers what fun these small Pipers can be. There's a slightly used one for sale here. Care to take a look?" he said, smiling at Freddie.

"Whoa, Bob, give the lady a chance to check out the ride first," Neil said as he helped her into the cockpit of his plane. There were a half-dozen other small private planes on the field. Neil's red one looked the newest and shiniest. It was reassuring to feel that this one had been carefully maintained. She still remembered her fears during her college years when she stepped into a date's old jalopy. If her father had been alive he would have had a fit to see her drive off in "that old piece of junk."

After slowly taxiing across the airfield, Neil pushed the throttle all the way in as he turned onto the runway. Freddie took a deep breath and shut her eyes. At lift-off, she opened them and unclenched her fists. A feeling of awe and exhilaration swept over her as she looked at the spectacle below. It was the same kind of excitement she had felt as a child when she sat atop the giant Ferris wheel for the first time and looked down at the toy-sized houses below

"Now I know what they mean when they describe this as a 'heart stopping' experience," she said as they returned after their brief flight. "Next time, I'd love to fly over my place and see how they're progressing on the shopping mall."

"I was worried about you at first," Neil said. "You were deadly pale when you climbed into that cockpit, but later when I saw you, looking below, you had rosy cheeks like a child. Didn't I tell you flying in a small plane was fun? Now let's go somewhere and celebrate."

From that day on, Freddie became addicted, and signed on with Bob Curcio for flying lessons. Learning to fly, even a tiny plane, was not easy, she soon found. The instrument panel seemed overwhelmingly complicated at first, but with Bob's patient guidance, she learned which button to use, and why.

"Above all," he cautioned, "Keep your cool, no matter what. Say, for some reason, your engine quits on you – that's not fun and games. But if that happens remember two things – one, stay calm, and don't panic; second, keep the plane *level.*" An airplane, he said, could be controlled even without engine power if it was handled like a glider. Bob's matter-of-fact manner was reassuring, though the thought of engine failure frightened her a little. For several weeks she continued her flying lessons. With each session her skill and confidence grew, until at last she was deemed ready to make her first solo flight.

Both Neil and Janine were at the airfield to watch her. "I feel as nervous as a bride," Freddie laughed as she climbed into the plane.

For fifteen minutes she soared above the Connecticut River valley, smoothly coordinating her rudder with her ailerons to carve smooth turns, all the while saying to herself, "I'm actually doing this, going to be a pilot!"

Then it happened.

The engine made some strange, popping sounds, then suddenly went silent.

Freddie did not remain calm, as Bob had advised. She went into a cold sweat. She almost forgot Bob's advice: *keep the plane level.* The horizon indicator on the instrument panel showed that the plane was level, thank God, but her slowing airspeed meant that she was gradually losing altitude. Below her, she saw that the houses and trees were looming ever closer. It was like being in a nightmare, but she knew it was real.

Suddenly a thought flashed through her mind. "Was there really a Hell?" A wave of long suppressed guilt swept over her. "Was a fiery crash going to be her personal Hell?"

But just as suddenly she spotted an opening on a fairly straight two-lane road not far ahead. She could see a group of several cars traveling in the same direction as she was headed. No traffic was coming from the opposite direction. Then she saw a slower moving truck somewhat ahead of the pack of cars. She figured the space between the cars and the truck was enough for her to land the plane, but that space was getting smaller as the faster cars made up the difference as they gained on the truck. She glanced again at her instrument panel and saw that she was still making 65 knots, faster than the cars were supposed to be going on that type of road. She was losing altitude too rapidly to look for another landing area. She had to go for it.

"Getty Oil," the name on the back of what turned out to be an oil tanker began to loom larger as Freddie tried to squeeze into the ever-shrinking space between the cars and the tanker truck.

"God! I may not deserve your help, but I need it now!" an inner voice screamed as she fought to keep the plane level against the turbulence the truck was leaving in its wake. She feared that the cars that were now just behind her, but below her, might not have seen her. Would they be able to stop in time?

A bump, followed by another, focused her mind again. She had landed, but she wasn't out of trouble. She pushed the brake hard, imagining the fiery disaster that would occur if she plowed into the tanker. She closed her eyes as "Getty Oil" filled her windshield.

For a second all was quiet. Then she realized that she was trembling all over, hands still clenched to the steering wheel. As she sat, ashen-faced, her body soaked with sweat, a heavy-set man rushed up to the side of the Piper.

"Are you OK, lady?" he asked. "I happened to see you in my mirror, just as you were coming and I stepped on it," he said. "Close call. You were sure lucky!"

In an effort to calm the situation with some humor, the driver added, "Did you run out of gas? I've got plenty in my truck!"

With that, Freddie tried to respond, but was so shaken that all she could manage was a twisted, one-sided smile as she opened the cockpit door and thanked the trucker for saving her life. She could barely climb out of the plane. When she did get out, she stepped on a small pebble, turned her ankle, pitched forward and broke her collarbone.

34

Media Darling

The local media gave Freddie high marks for her "heroism in safely landing her plane" and avoiding a crash in a populated area. A television reporter had a live interview with her in the hospital. (The scene of the emergency landing in the roadway had been shown just before the interview.)

"How did you feel when your engine conked out?"

What do you think? she thought. "Terrified," she said, "'til I remembered Bob Curcio's advice."

The *Newfield Bee* had gone all out in its coverage of one of its most well known citizens – Freddie was shown being lifted onto a stretcher and the plane was pictured alongside the road where it had been towed. The paper had used an old high school yearbook photo of Freddie as "the girl with the most cheerful nature." The accompanying story described her accomplishments as a cook and writer, and wound up by saying, *Fredrika's remarkable landing seems to have broken the Eliot family's history of bad luck.* The article cited the accidental deaths of her father and grandfather, the early passing of her mother and sister, and the recent fire in her woods at Eliot Farm.

Some readers, like Matthew Swenson, were amused. "The *Bee* never hinted that Freddie was like her father, who, without doubt, was the clumsiest man in town. She escapes a near fatal accident, then turns her ankle on a pebble and winds up in the hospital."

✶ ✶ ✶ ✶ ✶ ✶

As usual, there were rumors following the near crash, but aviation agency inspectors could find no cause for the engine failure. Freddie spent a few days in the hospital and returned home, where a number of letters and phone messages awaited her. Janine was very busy, attending to Freddie and answering the mail from friends and strangers who were congratulating Freddie on her courage and skill. It took a while before Freddie's nerves recovered from the trauma. Her beloved kitten, Oreo, proved to be the most effective medicine of all.

"Oreo's little engine never quits," Freddie said, as she felt the vibrations in his body as he purred. "I never cared much for cats, in fact I was a bit afraid of them, but this little creature is now my best friend. Except for you, Janine. You've been such an incredible help, in every way. Sometimes I suspect you must have had nurse's training."

Janine paused before answering. "As a matter of fact, I did attend nursing school for one year, then I had to quit because of my mother's illness." Her story was not entirely true. Janine had been caught stealing drugs from the hospital for her mother, who was an addict.

35

The Ultimate Lie

The weeks passed peacefully as the pressures from the newspaper and the publisher abated, and both women became less tense with each other. Teatime in the den had become a pleasant ritual. The subject of David had long been a taboo, but one afternoon, as she poured herself another cup of Earl Grey tea, Janine said, "I hear that David's doing fairly well in Hartford. That critic he's latched on to's been touting him as the next Van Gogh. A ridiculous comparison, of course. David's not crazy, like Van Gogh, but he's smart enough to know a sucker when he sees one. He's a leech, an opportunist. How lucky you were not to have married him. I'm glad I saved you from that!"

"Saved me! What do you mean? Did you do something to stop him from marrying me?" Freddie was outraged.

Janine smiled over her teacup. Smugly, she said, "Yes, it was easy. I simply told him that you and I were lovers."

✶ ✶ ✶ ✶ ✶ ✶

Strangely enough, Freddie's reaction had been one of shock, rather than anger at Janine's revelation. She was intelligent enough to know that – in certain circles, at least – she and Janine were probably suspect. Gays and lesbians were favorite topics of conversations, she knew, but to think that David would fall for such a lie surprised her. It was now too late to undo the damage. In any case, her feelings for him had changed. He no longer could hurt her.

Neil's reaction when she told him of Janine's intrigue was unsurprising. "Your loyalty to that woman continues to amaze me. Can't you see she's desperate to keep her hold on you? Your marriage would have wrecked all her plans." (He had been told that Janine was heiress to Freddie's estate.) "I am surprised, though, that David bought the story so easily. He may have been influenced by his mother, who you say looked at you in a funny way when you mentioned living with Janine. Much as I hate to agree with Janine on anything, she may have been right in calling David a leech. It takes one to know one. And don't worry about David gossiping. I suspect he might not want anyone to know that he'd been involved with a lesbian. Around here, we know it ain't true. We all know about your interest in *men*, though I don't seem to have made much progress in that respect." He laughed.

Ruefully, Freddie said, "It's a funny thing about me and men. I can't seem to get to the finish line with them. George, Patrick, then David. Of course, Al was to blame in two cases. For a long time I really hated her. Now I feel less vengeful."

As she spoke, Neil was still wondering why she continued to stick with Janine. After the latest episode, Freddie had every reason to throw her out, find herself another assistant. He sensed that Freddie was afraid of her. But why? he mused.

"Freddie, I'm sure you'd be happy to take a break from Janine right now. I've been looking at some travel brochures about cruises. Of course, they're never as glamorous as they look in the pictures – the sexy young girls are really overfed, middle aged matrons, and the lovely, deserted beaches are crawling with unattractive tourists, but it might be fun to try one. Are you game?"

Freddie laughed, "You must have read my mind. Two singles on an upper deck sounds perfect, doesn't it? Good food, lots of sun, and just ourselves for company. Let's run away from home together!"

36

Cruising

They boarded the ship, the Ocean Queen, in Miami a few weeks later. The '91-'92 winter in Connecticut was shaping up to be one of the worst on record, so Freddie and Neil were ecstatic to be in the warm sun of south Florida. Freddie – surprisingly enough – had no qualms about getting on a plane to fly to New York and then on to Miami. Her recent brush with death may have given her a feeling of immortality, but in any case, she and Neil enjoyed the two-hour flight from New York, spending almost the entire flight in animated conversation. Freddie, who never liked being in close proximity to strangers on a commercial flight, found that being pressed close to Neil in their economy-class seats was so stimulating that she found herself daydreaming of more intimate scenes on board ship – though she still managed to keep her end of the conversations going, not letting on what was really going through her mind! The thumping of the landing gear as it locked into position knocked out those daydreams and she and Neil prepared their seats and tray tables for landing. Freddie was disappointed that the flight was about to end, but then she starting thinking about the fun that was to come on board the Ocean Queen.

Once on board and settled into their cabins, they found that they had been assigned to a table at the eight o'clock sitting. As they explored the decks and took part in the mandatory lifeboat drill they noticed that they were atypical of many passengers. Most of them were young, romantic singles or older couples. Those in their age bracket were often families with young children, and they dined at the six o'clock sitting. Neil and Freddie were happy to have been spared the noise and confusion of toddlers or whiny, spoiled youngsters. They shared their table with a retired general and his wife, a pair of honeymooners and two young college girls. Estelle Brown, the general's wife, looked curiously at Freddie when they arrived at the table on the first evening at sea.

"Forgive my rudeness, but your face looks vaguely familiar. Could I have seen you on TV? That lovely red hair is so striking."

Freddie was uncomfortable and said nothing.

Mrs. Brown's face still had a puzzled look. She was not to be denied.

Finally Neil spoke up. "Yes. You may have seen her on TV. A couple of months ago she was involved in a somewhat miraculous escape from what would have been a fatal plane wreck."

Triumphantly, Estelle Brown cried, "That's it! You were being interviewed in the hospital, after you landed your crippled plane in the middle of a highway. That's what I call *aplomb*."

Freddie blushed as her tablemates stared her at her with renewed interest. "The media made a big fuss over it. It wasn't bravery or skill, just plain good luck. It's over now, and I'm just trying to forget it." Her words had the desired effect – curious though they were, the others took the hint and asked no questions.

Much of the time Freddie wore dark glasses as she strolled on the deck or sunned in a chaise around the edge of the swimming pool. She had long, exceptionally fine legs, which were usually hidden in slacks, and she was pleased to catch Neil's eyes as he looked her over.

"Freddie, you have a great pair of legs. I can see now why you were so anxious to show them off on a cruise," he said.

She laughed. "Unfortunately, I got short changed on the top portion of my body. Al, on the other hand was very well endowed. I wonder if you would have liked her." On the cruise she had felt much more relaxed, and was finally able to talk about her sister. She was also able to confide about other problems in her past. Neil had proved the perfect companion. He had grown a short, well-tended, brown beard for the trip that added interest to his face. She watched him as he leaned over the ship's rail, "What a nice looking, sweet man he is. What a shame I'm not in love with him," she thought wistfully.

✶ ✶ ✶ ✶ ✶ ✶

Janine's offer to meet them at Bradley International Airport had been turned down, so they arrived home by limo. Neither had made any attempt to disguise their coolness towards Janine as she tried to embrace them. After that she was being overly efficient as if to hide her embarrassment from their rebuff.

"You'll find a pile of letters waiting for you," she said. "I just couldn't keep up with them."

"Never mind that, how's little Oreo? I really missed him. Is he all right?"

"He's not so little anymore. Wait till you see how he's grown. He's been sleeping on your bed ever since you left. Neil, would you be going on to your place, or would you join us here for some coffee?"

"Thanks, but I'll be pushing on. There'll be a lot of business waiting for me, I hope." The very thought of drinking a cup of coffee with that bitch made him sick. Somehow, Freddie must be persuaded to get rid of her.

Freddie couldn't wait to run up to her bedroom to hug Oreo. He was not only a joy to see, but served as a buffer between herself and Janine. She delayed going into the kitchen as long as she could. Janine had brewed the coffee and had set two mugs and a plate of store-bought coffee cake on the kitchen table.

"Tell me," she said, "was it as wonderful as you'd hoped it would be? I must say, both of you look so tan and rested."

"Yes, in a sense it was a wonderful escape, but frankly, those gargantuan, floating palaces are overwhelming. You really need a road map to find one's way to the elevator or the dining room. The biggest excitement on the cruise came on the day a toddler got lost. The parents were in hysterics and all the passengers and the entire ship's company were anguished for several hours until the little boy was finally found, sound asleep in a linen closet. It was the only time when all of the passengers – and there were three thousand of us, of every color, size and shape – felt a common bond. I don't see how he could have fallen overboard – the railings are too high – but all of us must have felt the same dread."

Janine took a bite of the coffee cake. "Among the many calls that came while you were gone, one really intrigued me. It was from a Louise Henshaw, who's planning to open a bridal boutique in the new shopping mall." She gave a nervous laugh. "You and Neil aren't going to get married are you?"

"Heavens no! I like him even better after our cruise, especially with that cute beard, but I like him too much to marry him. I guess I'd better call her back and find out what gives."

37

A New Idea

Louise Henshaw, when reached on the phone, had a high-pitched, pseudo English accent. She explained that she had seen Freddie on TV and had read newspaper stories about her. Freddie disliked her pushy tone, but listened as the woman explained, "It occurred to me, that with your well-known cooking ability, as well as your well-known writings, and now with your recent celebrity, we might make a winning combination. Bridal gowns by Louise, bridal cakes by Freddie. Custom gowns and custom cakes. It said in the article that you'd studied bridal cake making. Is that true?"

"Yes," she admitted hesitantly. All that flattery sickened her. Her instinct told her to back off. Wedding cakes were great fun to create, but not under those auspices. "I'm sorry, but I'm not set up to operate on such a scale, but I'm honored that you thought of me," she said, as she quickly hung up the phone.

She was about to leave the kitchen when the phone rang again. It was Louise Henshaw, obviously a woman who couldn't take no for an answer, or was so thick-skinned that she didn't know curtness when it hit her. "We haven't even discussed price," she said. "May I come to your house and talk it over?"

This phony aristocrat wants to get her foot in my door, wants to see this house, thought Freddie. Be stern; don't let her manipulate you. "I'm afraid you didn't understand that I'm simply *not* interested." Plunk, down went the phone. "Well, I guess I've just made another enemy." She said to Janine. "The poor woman probably thought she was handing me a great opportunity. I should have told her that I don't need the money, but that would have sounded so crass, wouldn't it? Well, I think I'll go upstairs now and cuddle up with Oreo. He doesn't want anything from me but love."

※ ※ ※ ※ ※ ※

The coolness between the women gradually thawed, but it took a long time. What Janine had said to David – the lesbian lie – was appalling, and inexcusable, yet, in a way she felt relieved to have broken with David. Their marriage wouldn't have worked, she told herself. She tried to comfort herself by picturing the prim and prudish Emily Slocum Newcombe as her mother-in-law, his super snobbish brothers as her brothers-in-law, and her imagined father-in-law's badly concealed scorn of his sissy, artist son. To top it all, they would probably end up eating overcooked roast beef every Sunday with the Newcombe family in their musty, portrait hung, dining room. She always felt better after imagining such a scenario.

Neil had gone off to Vermont on a new job, designing a two-million-dollar log cabin for an ultra rich couple who wanted to "rough it" among the pines. With his absence, she felt restless. It had been such a happy experience working with him on the Langford house. He had often praised her for her color sense, and sometimes she daydreamed about becoming his assistant as a color coordinator. This was a job for an interior designer, not a mere amateur, she admitted. Subconsciously, what she really wanted to do was to escape from Janine. But, how?

Every day she tried to be out of the house as much as possible. Her social life had quickened since the plane incident, but after a while eating diet luncheons with friends became a bore and, without a man, planning little dinners at home became difficult. She had encouraged Janine to take a few days off, but that was only a brief respite from their deadly routine together.

"Have you ever thought of teaching a cooking course?" one of her friends once asked. Yes, she had. A teacher at the high school had suggested it. "You could make it something very special: just take on a few girls for a four- or six-session course. It would be fun for them, and for you, too."

The idea appealed, until she began to think of Janine. How far had those lies to David spread? She remembered the play, *The Children's Hour*, the story of two women teachers whose lives had been ruined by gossip. No, she was not ready to take that risk. And yet, she liked the idea of teaching a class in basic cooking.

To her delight, a new idea began to stir in her brain. Why not start a cooking course for *men?* The more she thought about it, the more excited she became. It could be called *For Gentlemen Only*.

38

For Gentlemen Only

At the *Newfield Bee* Rosie Winfred had a surprise visitor. Freddie came in to thank her for the recent article she had written about her. Typical of Rosie's style, it was far too gushy for Freddie's taste. "It was a lovely piece. I really didn't deserve it," she lied. Briefly, she described her recent cruise before coming to the point of her visit.

"As you know, I'm no longer writing. Guess I just ran out of words," she laughed. "But I'd very much appreciate your thoughts on a new project I'm thinking of starting – a cooking course for men. How do you like the title, *For Gentlemen Only?* Most men are great barbeque masters, but I know that some of them are actually closet cooks. With so many wives now working, I feel that a good many men would be interested in helping with some of the kitchen tasks and give their wives a break. Apart from that, I'd simply enjoy teaching five or six men the art of basic cooking. Nothing fancy. That could be added later. I'm gung-ho about the idea, but I wanted to get your opinion." She looked searchingly at Rosie, as if to ask her advice, though she'd already made up her mind to proceed with the project.

Freddie's trick worked. Rosie snapped at the bait. Two days later, in a column headed, *What's Freddie up to Now?* Rosie told about Freddie's visit "looking wonderfully rested after her recent cruise" and enthusiastically described her new project, "luring men into the kitchen."

The word "luring" was a bit strong, Freddie admitted, but never mind, the gossip column worked. A number of men called, anxious to hear more about the project. "I'm still in the process of putting it all together, but give me your name, and I'll give you more details later." She avoided saying the stale expression, "I'll get back to you."

Women also called. One of them playfully asked, "Does the course also teach them how to clean up afterward?"

✷ ✷ ✷ ✷ ✷ ✷

"Beware of what you wish for," Freddie said to Janine as they counted up the number of calls from would-be-cooks. The little column in the *Bee* had generated an astonishing amount of interest. There already were enough names on the list to start several small cooking classes. "Now what should I do? How can I organize this situation? I know about cooking, but I've never taught," she said.

With Janine's help, they checked out the basic essentials – the kitchen space, the number and types of courses to be offered, the cost of additional cooking utensils, and last, the price of the course per student.

"Teaching should be a snap for you. In a sense that's what your writing has been about," said Janine. Neither mentioned that in past years Janine had done much of the writing.

"I'm not looking to make money on this, but I don't fancy going broke," said Freddie as she watched Janine, who was skillfully totaling the final costs. Their work on the project had already served a vital purpose. It gave them a much-needed distraction from the personal problems between them. They had a mutual interest now, and the road ahead looked far more favorable.

✶ ✶ ✶ ✶ ✶ ✶

With a kitchen supply catalog at hand, Freddie was busy making her lists of new utensils needed when her phone rang. "Freddie, I'll bet you're surprised to hear from me," said a once-familiar voice. It was Matt Swenson. She had not spoken to him in years, since the day he came to report the gossip about her sister and Patrick Nelson. It seems he wanted to sign up for her cooking class.

"Knowing you, Freddie, I'm sure you'll make it fun. And who knows, I might even learn something about cooking," he said.

You have so many things to learn, Buster, she thought. Tact, for one. Having Matt in her class might be awkward, but she could not refuse him. "Yes, I'm surprised to hear from you and totally astonished at the response that's come from a few off-hand remarks I'd made to Rosie Winfred."

Matt laughed. "Come on, Freddie. You knew perfectly well what could happen when Rosie sniffs out a story. Talk about a skillfully planted idea!"

It was Freddie's turn to laugh. "All right, you've found me out. Now tell me the truth, why are you signing up for my course?"

Much of the amusement left Matt's voice as he told her about his coming divorce. "Yes, it's been a shock. After 12 years I thought I knew Gloria, inside and out. I guess I took her for granted, never dreamed that she would tire of me and start some extracurricular activity. So now I've moved to a bachelor's pad and have to fend for myself. I don't care about learning any fancy stuff, just enough to keep me alive. Think you can do this?"

What an irony, she mused, as she remembered Matt's warning about Patrick's double-dealings with Al. She, too, had taken Patrick for granted, and David, too, for that matter.

"Welcome to the club. Let's clear off the blackboard and get cooking!" She felt sad for Matt, but, in a sense, relieved to hear that others had also been tricked. "The price for the six two-hour sessions, will be $600, which will include the cost of the ingredients and a copy of my book, *Adventures in the Kitchen*."

✶ ✶ ✶ ✶ ✶ ✶

Matt Swenson was in the group of six men who posed with Freddie for a picture to celebrate the opening of *For Gentlemen Only*. Rose Winfred, who had claimed credit for the name of the course (untrue), was officiously rushing about the kitchen, notebook in hand, interviewing all of the students. Watching her, Freddie had worried that the woman's nosiness would annoy the men to the point of causing some to withdraw from the course, but all seemed pleased when the article and picture appeared in the *Bee* a couple of days later. Apparently, Matt had said nothing about the divorce. He was smart enough to know of "Nosy Rosie's" reputation.

Among the six men, only three had wives to cook for – Jeffrey Smith, a young banker, whose wife was a realtor; Alan Crimsky, an insurance broker, whose wife was a hair dresser, and Doug Sparkman, a writer, whose wife was a lawyer. They all had a common trait: a love for their wives, whom they hoped to help by sharing the chores in the kitchen.

Peter Hawley was the oldest in the group. Recently widowed after a marriage of over 50 years, he was a retired schoolteacher. He hated the idea of a community living, and wanted to be able to stay on in his small house.

"I was so helpless after Ruth died. Couldn't even boil an egg. Can't afford to eat out all the time, but I figured that I could survive if I learned how to cook for myself. Who knows,

I might even enjoy it," he said, smiling. He was a small, slightly stooped, gray-haired man. Freddie immediately loved him.

The other single man, Denis Lindstrom, startled Freddie when he sauntered into the kitchen. Her shock was so apparent that it caused him to laugh. "Mrs. Eliot, you look as if you'd seen a ghost. I must remind you of someone. Hope it was somebody you liked?"

She managed to stammer. "The voice is different, but the body build, the way you move, with your head bent forward a bit, is uncannily like him, even that shock of hair. I haven't seen him in years. He might be bald now, for all I know. It's been a long time."

"Ah, but you *liked* him, didn't you? Maybe there's hope for me."

"This is a cooking course, not a lonely hearts club," she said coolly. "By the way, I'm a 'Miss' not a 'Mrs.' And my friends call me Freddie."

The man reached into a chest pocket, pulled out a pair of glasses and inspected her carefully. "A 'Miss,' is it? I have a feeling we're going to be *very* good friends."

Inwardly Freddie recoiled. Patrick Nelson had charm. This man had all the appeal of a rattlesnake. He could mean trouble, she told Janine later.

39

Unwelcome Attention

Blake Jennings, at his desk at the *Newfield Bee,* was perplexed. A letter from one of his readers demanded an answer and he did not know what to do. Perhaps his friend Freddie might help.

"This is a delicate matter, something I can't discuss on the phone. Could you tear yourself away from your 'gentlemen' friends and drop in to see me?"

When she arrived a few hours later, he showed her the letter. "This belongs in the 'cries of outrage' file," he said.

For years, the writer complained, she had been supporting a modest, but worthy charity, the *Open Door,* which distributes presents at birthdays and at Christmas to residents of local nursing homes. She had made her annual contribution a few weeks before Christmas, then hardly a few weeks later, had received a begging letter from the organization, asking for further funds so they could take advantage of "buyer opportunities in the future."

Jennings agreed with the writer that it seemed like an odd, if not suspicious, way of raising funds. "Freddie, you've been involved with that charity, and I see that your friend, Janine Fulton's the treasurer. Is it possible that the letter had been sent in error?"

"Absolutely!" Freddie replied quickly. "Janine will feel terribly to learn of her mistake. You see, she's been swamped with work, trying to help me launch the cooking course. I'm sure she could send you a tactful reply to that reader's complaint. That letter was probably written for *next* year's fund campaign. Sometimes I suspect her of being too well organized, of planning too far ahead."

She attempted a laugh as she said it, but she was dismayed. The editor had given her a copy of the letter, which she later showed to Janine. It was hard to tell if the distress was real or faked, she thought, as Janine cried out, "Oh, this is terrible! It makes us look like con artists. I'll send a letter to the paper immediately."

✶ ✶ ✶ ✶ ✶ ✶

Janine's letter, written with her customary skill, did not entirely calm Blake Jenning's suspicions. As he told Donald Bailey when they lunched together two days later, "What is it about that Janine friend of Freddie's? She's not gay, I'm sure. I don't buy those lesbian rumors that float around from time to time. Both of them have track records with men, but somehow I feel uneasy about Janine. She's attractive, and all that, but I don't feel comfortable about her. The letter, by the way, was very well written, much in the style of Freddie when she wrote those weekly columns for me. Hmmm . . . You don't suppose Janine could actually have written some of those pieces?"

Bailey laughed. "I don't know about the writing – that's your field of expertise. Freddie Eliot's been my friend and client ever since her father died twenty-five years ago, and I believe in her completely. As for that charity that Janine talked Freddie into supporting, *Open Door*, I was wary of it at first, but it turned out to be legit. Poor Freddie's been unlucky with the men in her life.

Jennings paused as he signed the bottom of the lunch check. "How about her last boyfriend – the artist? What ever happened to their plan about starting an art gallery together? She was so keen on it, and on him, too?" He laughed. "Now I'm sounding like a gossipy old biddy."

✶ ✶ ✶ ✶ ✶ ✶

Financially, the cooking course had been disappointing. The cost of the new utensils and the meal ingredients had been higher than projected, but Freddie was so happy that she did not care. Money was no problem, and her income from her share of the shopping mall leases (two percent of the shop rentals) increased as the mall grew. The men in the class proved to be a congenial group who enjoyed the two hours together as much as Freddie did.

She still disliked Denis Lindstrom, the Patrick look-alike, but she had learned how to ignore his insinuating remarks, and gradually he gave up trying to impress her with his so-called charm. The old teacher, Peter Hawley, was her favorite. After each class, if there were any extra food, she would pack it up as a "doggy bag" for him. The other men pretended not to notice, as they too, had become fond of the elderly man.

At the opening session the class had sat around the huge kitchen table, drinking coffee or tea, and sampling some of Freddie's famous cakes as she gave a humorous, ten-minute lecture on the basic elements of cooking and demonstrated the various utensils and how to use them. As she passed the ingredients and the tools around, she said, "To start our course, we're going to make a wonderful, big pot of chicken and vegetable soup, which you can take home to enjoy."

Each man was given a cutting board and a knife suitable for the ingredient he was to prepare. "Cutting and chopping is one of the greatest skills of a chef," she said, as she supervised each student. The old man had a problem with his arthritic fingers, so he needed special attention. "You may have to do it a little more slowly, but you'll master it," she said. He smiled gratefully.

In the middle of the class she realized, with chagrin, that the chicken pieces may have been cut too large to be fully cooked in the allotted time. "I think I may have talked to you to long," she apologized. "We may have to continue for a half hour longer. The soup will be worth waiting for, I promise you."

And indeed it was, according to the reports from the group when they met two days later. The "Gentlemen Only" was off to a very promising start, and Janine and Freddie were at peace with each other.

✷ ✷ ✷ ✷ ✷ ✷

To Freddie, some of the most rewarding aspects of the course were the phone calls from grateful wives. "Jeffrey surprised me on Sunday morning with the most delicious eggs benedict I've ever eaten." Another lauded her husband's apple pie, and another wife thanked Freddie for "teaching Doug how to clean up afterwards. It was astounding! My kitchen used to look like a battlefield after he'd finished 'helping' me."

Matt Swenson, whom she had not been too happy to have in her class, was surprisingly tactful and helpful in every way. Perhaps the recent failure of his marriage had taught him something, Freddie mused. When the course ended he called to thank her.

"Your course was fun, as I knew it would be, but more important, it helped my confidence, which was at an all-time low. Right now, I'm no great chef, but I was wondering if you'd care to come over and be my first dinner guest."

Freddie tactfully explained that she'd devised a rule to avoid singling out "teacher's pets." Actually, it was aimed at stopping gossip, a sort of "no fraternizing" rule between teacher and student. She was glad to have a valid excuse to turn him down. "But we'll always be good friends," she promised.

One of Matt's most helpful contributions to her had been his skill at deflecting Denis Lindstrom's odious insinuations. Matt seemed to sense her feeling about the man and tried to intercept Denis when he grew too impertinent, or too conceited. The sauce-making class could lend itself to his sassy comments. "Freddie, would you call yourself a 'saucy lassie'?" Or else he'd parade his erudition: "There's no sauce in the world like hunger – Cervantes."

"Can it, Denis. We all know how smart you are," Matt would sneer.

It was difficult to humble such a man, but Matt succeeded in making life easier for Freddie. He also made a point of staying in the kitchen with Freddie until she was rid of Denis. "If that man ever gives you trouble, let me know," he said, as he hugged her after the final class.

As she feared, the end of the course did not mean the end of Denis' attentions. A few days later, the phone call came. "Thanks to you, I've just made a fabulous meal, and I'd love to share it with you. How about it?" The nerve of the man! His voice indicated that he'd expected her to say 'yes.'

"Sorry, but I made it a rule not to socialize with my students."

"Bet you just made up that rule to get rid of guys like me. Come on, I'm not your student any longer. What's wrong with me? Some women would jump at a chance to have dinner at my place," he whined.

"Well, let 'em jump." She slammed down the receiver.

40

Obsession

Denis Lindstrom, the spoiled only-child of wealthy parents, was angry. Who did this woman think she was? At her age, she should be glad to have an invitation from an attractive bachelor. Denis, at 39, still had a callow look. There was a petulance about his mouth, derived no doubt from striving to get his way. Don't deny me, or you'll regret it, his expression said.

Most men would have taken Freddie's reply as a hint, and backed off. But her rebuff only made him more eager to win her over. The more he thought about her, the more he became obsessed by her. He had lots of time for the conquest, as he was a freelance writer. Two or three times a day he would drive his Mercedes past her house, hoping to track her, and at night he'd watch her windows, spying on her as she undressed for bed. None of this was really exciting. Porn movies were better. But it was her very resistance to his charm that stimulated him. Once in a while he would phone her, then lose his nerve and hang up. He thought about her constantly, even dreamed about her. But even in the dreams she turned him down.

One morning he encountered her in the super market and was so flustered that he could barely mutter a "hello" as he hurried past. Freddie was perplexed. The cocksure, cheeky young man had suddenly turned shy. What was going on?

✶ ✶ ✶ ✶ ✶ ✶

Peter Hawley, the retired teacher, was also smitten by Freddie, and not afraid to show it. Three months after the course ended he appeared at her door, a large, flat box in his hands.

He was looking less frail and pale. Obviously, his newfound cooking skills agreed with him. He followed her into the kitchen and placed the box on the table, then opened it, grinning all the while.

"Yesterday was my son's birthday, and I entertained him and his family, six of us in all, with a turkey dinner. I just had to bring you these leftovers to show off. Just as you said, cooking a turkey isn't hard at all. Making the proper dressing was a little trickier, and getting the sauce to come out nice and smooth was harder. Sorry that my candied yams were all eaten up, and the creamed spinach, too."

He watched her proudly. She obviously enjoyed his offering. "If I weren't so selfish, I'd call Janine to come in and share this with me. Peter, I'm giving you four stars for this. As a teacher, you know how exciting it is to find a promising student." He blushed very red as she hugged him. Her friendship with Peter had been one of the most rewarding aspects of her cooking class. He seemed like a grandfather to her. Her own grandfather, famous in town as "Big Al," had died before she was born. He had had an overwhelming personality, she was told. This old man had a gentleness, a sweet nature, which she would have loved in a grandfather. It took her very little time to consider herself his adopted granddaughter.

During the classes he had watched Freddie as she tried to ignore the impertinence and boorish advances of Denis Lindstrom. "Is that guy Lindstrom still pestering you?" he asked. "I never liked the way he looked at you."

She laughed, "He tried to talk me into trying some of his home cooking, but I gave him the brush-off. I think he was really shocked that I hadn't fallen for his charm."

"I've lived a long time, so forgive me if I butt in with some advice. Be careful how you treat this man. A scorned man could be just as dangerous as a scorned woman."

✱ ✱ ✱ ✱ ✱ ✱

Denis Lindstrom lived in a fairly small house on the fringe of Newfield. For a man of his apparent means, it was modest. His silver Mercedes was the only clue to his wealth, and now he wished that he'd bought a less showy car. It would be much more difficult to follow Freddie in that vehicle. As the days passed his fixation grew, and he worried about it. Why should this rather average looking woman turn him into a brainless neurotic? He knew that his daydreams (and night dreams, too) were impossible to fulfill, but he had lost control, and knew it. Perhaps he should visit a shrink? No, it would be too mortifying. What would his parents think? They had already paid out plenty to keep him in a private sanitarium when he had gotten into a jam for molesting that woman in the movie theater.

Money was the answer, and he had plenty of it. Perhaps he should buy a less conspicuous car, maybe a pick-up truck? There were loads of them around Newfield. He felt quite elated as he drove towards a used car lot.

"I'm looking for a small van or truck that I can use on camping trips," he told the salesman. "No, I don't want any of those fancy jobs, just something simple. How about that tan one, over there?" It was a nondescript van with a small sign, *J & R Plumbers*, on both sides.

"This one will get you there and back, but wouldn't you rather – "

Lindstrom interrupted, "No, that one'll do. Any discount for cash?"

✷ ✷ ✷ ✷ ✷ ✷

Freddie had not seen Lindstrom or his Mercedes for some time and felt relieved. There had been days when she had the uneasy feeling of being followed. It was just a feeling, nothing tangible. One evening, as she was getting ready for bed, she saw beneath her window a vague shape moving in the bushes. She quickly pulled down the shades, and later made it a habit each evening to draw them in the other rooms as well.

Janine laughed at her. "Freddie, you're acting like a paranoid old maid. Granted that Denis was obnoxious during the classes, it doesn't make him a stalker."

"I've never pretended to have psychic powers, but there's something creepy about that man. Have you noticed how often we've had phone calls with nobody on the other end?" said Freddie.

"Next thing you know, you'll be hearing heavy breathing," teased Janine. "Freddie, you've been looking at too much trash on the TV."

Though Janine tried to calm her, Freddie was still full of fears and told Neil about them when she saw him a few weeks later. He listened with concern, and believed her. She was not the emotional type of woman who would fantasize about such things.

"Tell me dear, what does this man look like? You say he's easy to identify. Very tall, lots of dark curly hair, and he drives a flashy, silver Mercedes sedan?"

They did not know that, as they were speaking, Denis Lindstrom was sitting in his mud-colored van, a few hundred yards away. A floppy golf hat covered his abundant hair and his hooded eyes were concealed behind dark glasses.

Lindstrom had seen Neil Walsh entering the Eliot house and was dismayed. For weeks he had been tailing Freddie and had seen no man in her life. Perhaps he shouldn't have worried. The man didn't look like a threat. He was shorter than Freddie, and certainly not handsome. Nothing special, really, but he didn't like the way Freddie greeted him as he arrived on the front porch. A bit too affectionately.

※ ※ ※ ※ ※ ※

Neil Walsh's appearance had changed Lindstrom's fantasies. Now he pictured Freddie in a different way, a more sensual one. He began using the telephone again. This time he did not simply hang up when she answered, but set off on a campaign of dirty talk. "Well, I see you have a new boyfriend. Good for you." He then would proceed with a litany of foul sexual acts "that the two of you are doing together. Aren't you the lucky ones?" At the first call Freddie was too shocked to hang up on him, but as the calls continued she learned to hang up immediately at the sound of his voice. Even when he knew that she'd hung up, Lindstrom lay alone in his darkened bedroom, with the phone in one hand, and continued his filthy monologue until he achieved climax.

※ ※ ※ ※ ※ ※

At other times he would drive around in his van, tracking Freddie, and occasionally, Neil. No longer did he hang around the Eliot house hoping for a naked view of Freddie. The drawn blinds defeated him.

He would have been delighted to see how outraged and frightened Freddie became when she received one of those obscene calls. At first, she told no one, not even Janine, about them. She felt soiled and violated. The man clearly was a nut case, but what could she do to stop him? He was not, like so many of such callers, anonymous. Knowing exactly who he was just made it worse.

When they heard about the calls, both Janine and Neil had the same logical suggestion – change your phone number and notify the police. She agreed to have her number changed, but the idea of calling the police appalled her. Her classes and her life on the whole had been going so well, that she didn't want all the publicity that an incident with the police would bring.

"Hold it, I think I have a friend who can help you. His name is Tim Dorrance, a retired policeman, who's very competent and above all, discreet," said Neil.

41

The Private Eye

"Private eye" was a term Tim Dorrance did not like – though that's just what he was. On TV private eyes were always shown as sleazy, foul-mouthed characters, whose ethics were suspect. Despite his years on the force, Dorrance still had the look of the choirboy he had once been, with his round blue eyes and a disarmingly childlike grin. The call from his old friend, Neil Walsh, excited him. The prospect of trapping a sexual pervert was enticing, even if it meant taking on the case at lower than his usual rate. He wasted no time checking on Denis Lindstrom's past.

"Neil, I'm glad you called me. That dirty talk on the phone indicated that the caller was abnormal, some kind of a freak who got his kicks saying obscene things to women. They seem to prefer picking on single women, or women alone. I looked up his record and found that this same man was put away in some fancy sanitarium for feeling up a dame in a movie theater. Spent six months in so-called rehab in '88. His wealthy family picked up the tab, and hired a gee-whiz lawyer to save him from jail. For the past five years since, his record's been clean, though the police have been keeping an eye on him."

Tim began his surveillance as he parked his old Dodge near the Lindstrom house and casually strolled around the area. Lindstrom, who looked just as he had been described by Freddie, was standing near the open door of his two-car garage, his silver Mercedes inside. Parked in the driveway was an old van belonging to some plumber, who was evidently doing some work inside the home. Tim soon returned to his car. He had seen enough. If that man were truly a stalker, as Freddie seemed to feel that he was, he would be a cinch to nab.

✶ ✶ ✶ ✶ ✶ ✶

Hiring Tim Dorrance had brought relief to Freddie – and to Neil, too, though Neil never told her about Lindstrom's past. Why further upset her? Changing a phone number was a real pain, he knew, but the peace of mind was worth it. Freddie had lost much of her tenseness and it showed in the relaxed look around her mouth and jaws. No longer did she jump at the sound of the phone.

One sunny Saturday in spring, as they ate brunch at the local diner, Neil suggested, "It's such a perfect day. I think we both need a change. How would you feel about running down to New Haven to check on Neil at Yale? They're having a two-day swimming meet, and I'd love to watch him in action. Could you stand all that splashing and screaming and whistle blowing?"

Freddie smiled. "You don't make it sound very inviting, but I'd love to meet that son of yours. Give me an hour to pack a small bag, and I'm yours for the weekend."

What did she mean by *yours*, Neil wondered.

Lindstrom, who had tailed them when they left the diner, was confused. He watched Freddie as she left Neil's red Pontiac and went into her house. A red car was a joy to follow, much easier than Freddie's big gray Olds. He hoped that Neil would return later and pick her up in his car. From their body language when they left each other, with rushed pecks on the cheeks, he had sensed that they would meet again soon. And he was right.

* * * * * *

There was considerable traffic on the road to New Haven, and even though the red Pontiac zigzagged from lane to lane, Lindstrom had no trouble tailing it. New Haven was fairly near Newfield and it was not long before they arrived and parked in the lot of a downtown hotel. He watched them as they walked through the entrance, each carrying a small bag. Holding a newspaper over his face, Lindstrom sat in the crowded lounge for about an hour, as he watched them sign in waited for them to come out of the elevator and exit the hotel. At the reception desk business had subsided, and Lindstrom approached the younger of the two clerks.

He pretended to be checking his watch as he said, "I'm supposed to be meeting a friend here, but she seems to have been delayed. Do you have a Miss Fredrika Eliot registered here? She's a friend from Newfield."

The young clerk opened the register and ran one finger down the list. "No, there's no Fredrika Eliot here, but there's a couple from Newfield, a Mr. And Mrs. Neil Walsh. Maybe you know them?"

"Idiot!" exclaimed the other clerk, after Lindstrom had walked away. "We pride ourselves on *discretion* here. You had no business opening your yap about other guests. Did you notice the look on that guy when you blabbed about the Walshes? He looked as if somebody had just shot his mother."

* * * * * *

There was no further reason for Lindstrom to remain in New Haven. The worst had happened. His prey had found a protector. Suddenly, Freddie seemed no longer the unattainable, fascinating woman to be pursued. From the moment he heard the word *Mrs.* the chase became pointless. She was no longer a fantasy, a virginal image in his mind, but plain Mrs. Walsh. At least that was the way it looked on the books. Strangely enough, after the first shock passed, he felt a lightness within him, as if some foul smelling thing had been lifted from him. He suddenly wanted to get away from Newfield and its unwholesome memories, but where?

Mexico had always been one of his favorite places. When he got home he would call his travel agent. What's the use of being a freelance writer, if you can't live a freelance life?

42

Lovers

As they drove home Sunday evening, Neil chose a back road to avoid traffic. Sitting close beside him, with her left hand on his thigh, Freddie asked, as they passed a lonely, deserted area, "Darling, what would you do if we suddenly had a flat tire?"

He laughed. "What a question! Why, I'd simply jack it up and put on the spare. It's no big deal."

Freddie began to giggle uncontrollably. Neil pulled over to the side of the road as Freddie started to get hysterical. It took her a few minutes before she calmed down and wiped her eyes with a Kleenex. "Sorry, but I've been so happy, on such a high all weekend. I just remembered something silly, and it set me off." She did not say what it was, and Neil was smart enough not to ask. The ludicrous incident with David and the tire was best left unmentioned. Better change the subject, she thought.

"I loved your son, Neil. Looks like a taller, beardless, version of you. He was a little shyer than I imagined he would be, but he may have been a bit nervous about meeting me, or about me meeting him. His girlfriend was attractive, but couldn't she say anything more interesting than 'wow' every five minutes?"

The four of them had had a steak dinner after the meet on Saturday. It was a nondescript restaurant, but the famous *Morey's* was impossible to get into without a reservation. Neil promised Freddie "Next time we'll reserve a table. The place is legendary, and the food isn't bad, either."

When they returned to their hotel Neil picked up the room key at the desk. It was an older hotel and had not switched to king-sized beds. A popular arrangement for couples (and entire families) was a large room, furnished with a pair of double beds. When she had first seen the room, Freddie had laughed and said, "Mine, his, and *ours*. *W*hich is it going to be?" That night, after a tentative start, the question was soon answered, and both were as happy as newlyweds.

✶ ✶ ✶ ✶ ✶ ✶

They had decided, when they arrived home, to be discreet about their hotel stay together. Janine's jealousy would only grow if she knew of their change from friends to lovers.

"Why do you care about Janine's opinion? You're an adult. You don't have to be beholden to her for anything." (Or does she, Neil wondered.) "I can tell you one thing for sure, I won't spend a night with you in that house if that woman's there."

Freddie understood. A future as Neil's wife would be impossible unless she could rid herself of Janine – forever. But how? Janine knew too much about her. Yet, on the other hand, Freddie was not lily white either. She had allowed Janine to become too dominant, especially in money matters. Freddie decided to play a larger role in the management of her own checkbook. The recent incident about the fund appeal for the *Open Door* had re-awakened her suspicions. Janine was treasurer of that charity and of the *Day in the Country* as well. How much of those funds were actually used to operate those organizations? Only Janine had control of the bank accounts. The volunteer helpers adored her, were in her thrall. They were naïve, hardly likely to question any of her actions.

At first she planned to question Janine, but as usual she decided to avoid a confrontation. A headline in the *Bee* distracted her. Over the weekend, while she and Neil were in New Haven, a number of burglaries had taken place in town. There were no spectacular items taken, no large sums of money, no important pieces of jewelry. The burglar had sneaked into houses through unlocked windows on ground floors and had made off with a number of expensive cameras, computers and camcorders.

"Thank you, Tim!" exclaimed Freddie aloud when she read the news. Tim Dorrance had been adamant about checking all her lower windows. Newfield residents were luckier than those in Greenwich, a town of notoriously wealthy people, who had been victims of a cat burglar who stole the jewels from their bedrooms as they ate dinner below. Apparently, Newfield's "cats" couldn't climb to the second floor.

Apart from all the easily fenced electronic items there was little of real value in the Eliot house, though it was, in a sense, the most impressive house in town. A band of teenagers were probably the culprits, she thought. She was much more concerned about the stalker. On the road to New Haven she had had an eerie feeling that they were being followed, but saw no sign of Denis and his Mercedes. Yet, on the return drive home, she had no such feeling. She was tempted to tell Neil about it, as they drove home, but decided against it. "Leave those worries to Tim. He'll watch out for you. That's what he's being paid for," he'd probably say.

Three days later, Tim called to report that he had cased the Lindstrom property again and it "looks as if the guy's gone away. Don't know for how long, but I'll keep an eye on the place."

43

Tea with Janine

Freddie felt far less nervous, and she was perfectly happy to continue paying Tim his modest fee. He needed the money more than she. A few days later she and Janine had a really edifying conversation together. It was a quiet afternoon, no classes were scheduled. They were seated together on the couch in the den, drinking tea.

"Janine, I once remember you saying you'd forgiven your mother for all the harm she'd done to you. Do you still believe that, even though she's still selfish and demanding? And have you forgiven your husband for the five years of agony that he put you through?"

"Strangely enough, I've somehow managed to rid those past evils from my mind. You see I haven't been an angel myself." Janine confessed how she had been kicked out of nursing school, and later from the Peace Corps.

"The Peace Corps! What happened there?" asked Freddie.

Janine laughed. "I guess I didn't know I was supposed to live like a nun," she said. "The regional director and I got involved. End of story."

They sat in silence for a while. Janine's confessions were not entirely surprising to Freddie. "My life seems so drab compared with yours. I've never had an abusive husband, an unpredictable mother and a number of careers. I've never been to India, and probably never will. I've just sat here, in this old house, while people were dying, one by one – my mother, father, Aunt Gretchen and then my sister Alberta. A dreary life story, isn't it?"

"Your sister's sudden death must have been terrible for you," Janine said sadly. She paused, waiting to hear more. They were silent. Then Freddie said, "Yes, the worst part is that I could have saved her."

"What are you getting at? How could you have saved her?"

"By allowing her leave me. By not stopping her from joining Patrick in Chicago."

"But he was *your* fiancé wasn't he?" Janine asked.

In tears, Freddie explained how Al had wanted to leave the teahouse, asked her sister to buy her out, how she had refused and how they wound up hating each other. "Al got so tensed up, I think it killed her. You know. I can't hate her any longer. Or Patrick, too, for that matter. Al had an amazing affect on men. It's too late to forgive Al, but sometimes I wish I could forgive Patrick for cheating on me. He couldn't help himself, I know that now."

"Where is Patrick now? Would you feel better if you could meet him, and talk with him? It might be a wonderful thing for both of you. Perhaps you both need to forgive each other. I used to work in the same firm with Patrick, but barely knew him. After the Peace Corps trouble, I kept hands off men, but I might be able to locate him for you. Would you like me to try?"

44

The Letter

Until she met his look-alike, Denis Lindstrom, Freddie had seldom thought about Patrick in recent years, but after her confidences with Janine she could hardly get him out of her mind. How wonderful it would be to talk to him again, to travel the road toward forgiveness. True to her word, Janine had contacted Patrick's parent insurance firm in Hartford and had managed to find out Patrick's Chicago address.

Freddie's hand shook as she held the slip of paper from Janine with Patrick's address written on it. "What can I say to him? I want to sound friendly, but not too anxious. Janine, you're better at this than I am."

Between the two of them, they cobbled together a letter.

> *Dear Patrick,*
> *So much has happened in the years since we last saw each other, and I've thought of you so often. Have you married? Do you have a family? How is*

> your career progressing? Do you ever get a chance to travel east? Questions, questions!
> It would be such fun to see you again! Do let me know if you're passing this way.
>
> As ever,
Freddie
>
> P. S. I'm not married, but ever hopeful!

The letter was handwritten by Freddie on note-sized, French blue stationery and handed to Janine, who promised to mail it at once. The guilt about her part in Al's death had troubled her for years. Now she felt a release. The prospect of squaring things with Patrick excited her. How would he react when he saw her again? She studied her face in the mirror. There were no signs of gray in her hair, her jaw, however looked less firmly defined, and there were tiny wrinkles at the corner of her eyes, but on the whole, the years had not done too much damage. She did not need a dye job, but a facial would bring a glow to her skin, she decided, and while she was at it, she would check her wardrobe. It would take several days before she had a response to the letter, she mused. There was no hurry, she told herself, yet she rushed to ready herself (and the house) for the meeting. After the facial and the purchase of some new clothes, she started a massive house cleaning.

"I never saw you look so excited," Janine teased her. "Calm down. It may be weeks – or months – before he shows up. And who knows if he'll show up at all."

Freddie tried to act normal. She knew how silly she must have looked as she rearranged the furniture, constantly vacuumed and dusted, all the while looking for any imperfection in a room. Every day she eagerly checked the mail and felt her spirits drop when she found no letter. After a while, she was starting to lose the energy and high spirits that she once had felt, and her happiness had changed to irritation.

"Why don't you go out for a change, have lunch with a friend? All this waiting's tearing you down," Janine said.

The answer was always the same, "I have to stay home. I might get a call from Patrick. I thought I'd hear from him by now. How long has it been, six weeks? Are you sure you mailed that letter?" She was beginning to suspect that Janine had never mailed it. She was an odd one. One could not tell what went on in Janine's mind.

"Of course I mailed it. Why would I lie to you?" said Janine indignantly. "I've told you three times that I mailed the letter."

45

Manhattan

Day by day, the tension between them grew, and Freddie became increasingly distrustful of Janine. She had ignored the warnings from her lawyer and banker when she gave Janine so much control of her life. It was so pleasant to turn over the nitty-gritty financial details to a capable, congenial companion. "Numbers are not my thing," she would say to Janine, as if in apology for her indifference. Actually, Freddie was just plain lazy, not as helpless and stupid as she seemed.

It was time, she thought, to take a hard look at her finances. Janine had handled all the mail, paid all the bills, taken care of the correspondence. Her power of attorney entitled her to make out checks and to sign them. Freddie never looked at the monthly bank statements or attempted to balance her account.

On impulse – one day when Janine was out – Freddie looked in her checkbook. She was particularly interested in the stubs made out to Linda Sherman. For months the checks had been made out for three thousand dollars then, without explanation, the sum was raised to four thousand. This had been going on for six months, it seems. Ordinarily, Janine would explain the reason for a raise: "Mom needs a new wheelchair," or "Mom has to have eye surgery" and Freddie okayed the difference. Now, this was the real proof of Janine's deceitfulness. Janine was not only dishonest, but cruel, too. She must have been lying about mailing the letter. Why was Janine stringing her along for all these weeks, fueling her hopes that she might see Patrick again? That was almost as hurtful to her as the discovery of Janine's entries in the checkbook.

Obviously, Janine was up to some trickery and something must be done to investigate it. Going to New York to check out the real – or fake – Mrs. Sherman might be complicated. Janine was aware of how much Freddie hated the city, so Freddie had to find an excuse to go there.

"I had a call from Angela White. The poor thing's going in for cancer surgery. I'll have to run in and see her. I'll take an early train and be back by evening," she said.

Linda Sherman's address was familiar. She had often mailed checks to 1120 West End Avenue. It was a long, expensive taxi ride from Grand Central Station, but Freddie gladly paid the fare. She was unfamiliar with the New York bus and subway systems and didn't want to waste time getting lost on the wrong route.

The Sherman apartment was in one of those buildings built at the turn of the century when New York's West Side was briefly fashionable. In later years European refugees and Columbia University academics had favored the district. Comparable apartments on the East Side of Manhattan were far more expensive. The yellow-brick face of the building looked strongly built, but there was a dreariness about it, like a dowager's faded, old mink coat. The former doorman had been replaced years ago by a push button door operation in a cramped vestibule. Among the brass mailboxes Freddie located the name "L. Sherman."

She was apprehensive as she pushed the Sherman button. What sort of woman would she find? Janine had described her as a selfish, broken-down, former drunk and addict. Freddie held her breath as she waited for the click, click, click of the automatic door lock release mechanism. Nothing happened. She tried again, waited a few moments and pressed the button gain. Perhaps the old woman was lying dead on the floor of her place, alone and stinking. Maybe she was at the grocery store. Perhaps there was no such woman. Fear sent sweat trickling down Freddie's armpits. Finally she spotted the name "Grazio, Super." And pressed the button next to it. Nothing happened. After three tries she was ready to give up when suddenly the door opened. An olive-skinned, surly looking man in paint-stained coveralls stood before her. He obviously was not pleased at having been interrupted in his work.

"Yes? What you want?" he asked sourly.

"I came to see Mrs. Linda Sherman," Freddie stammered.

"She not here," he growled as he started to pull the door shut. "She in nursing home. Daughter come pick up mail."

Ah, that might explain the extra cost, Freddie thought. But why didn't she tell me?

She pulled the door open before it locked again and followed the man across the dingy lobby.

Determined to see the place, she suddenly remembered a card from Leslie Jenks that she'd tucked away in her purse. It looked a bit worn, but never mind, she thought, it could get me into the apartment. She caught up with the man and held out the card.

"I'm in real estate, and I'd like to see the apartment."

He looked dubious until she handed him a twenty-dollar bill. Grudgingly he said, "Follow me."

They rode the elevator to the third floor. The hallway looked even more dismal than the lobby. Pulling out a large bunch of keys, the superintendent pressed a light switch as he led her into the apartment.

"When go just close door," he said grumpily. The twenty-dollar tip had not improved his disposition.

Freddie turned on another light. As the room faced directly onto an interior courtyard it was very gloomy. The light revealed a surprisingly modern living room. She had not expected to find Swedish-modern furnishings in an elderly woman's apartment. In the bedroom she found another surprise: a modern, king-size bed that occupied most of one wall. There was no old lady's usual clutter here. The furniture was sparse: a pair of night tables, a long dresser, one comfortable armchair, and in one corner a small dressing table and bench. For an older woman there was a surprisingly large number of beauty aids on the dressing table: three or four lipsticks, mascara, eye shadow and a large bottle of perfume – "Tabu," one of Janine's favorites. Another of Janine's favorite beauty creams, Caress, was also on the table. Janine was very proud of her beautiful hands. She was faithful in creaming them twice each day – morning and night – with Caress. Freddie recalled how she had hated it when Janine had insisted on rubbing the powerfully scented cream on her collarbone when she was recuperating after the accident. Caress indeed!

A double-sized closet on one wall was closed by a pair of louvered doors. By this time Freddie was not that surprised when she found two terrycloth robes in his and her sizes. The larger one was big enough to wrap around as burly a man as Jim Bankson.

Freddie plopped herself down in the armchair. She was not entirely shocked. Janine and Jim had been buddies for a long time, and Janine had made no claims about her virtue, past or present. It was Janine's blatant deceit about her mother – the monthly extortion scheme that infuriated her. How many of her other "charities" did Janine skim from? For a long time Freddie had been suspicious of those monthly three-day stays in town with her "needy" mother. To catch her in such a brazen con game was too much. What to do?

✷ ✷ ✷ ✷ ✷ ✷

Before she left New York Freddie made a brief visit to her sick friend, Angela White. She did not stay long, just long enough to be able to say to Janine, without fibbing, "I'm so glad I had a chance to see Angela before her operation. The poor thing was so appreciative of my visit. She knows how I hate New York."

On her way to Grand Central she had stopped off at Saks and bought two blouses and a skirt. That would indicate that she'd spent some time shopping, not snooping. At the station she had time before her evening train to treat herself to supper at the Oyster Bar. Wistfully, she recalled the past when she and Al and their father had eaten there after their annual visit to FAO Schwarz' fabulous Christmas toy exhibit. Life was less fun now. And far more complicated.

46

Hatching Plans

By the time she arrived home it was so late that – to her relief – she barely had time to speak to Janine before going to bed. It was a day that she would long remember. A day in which a curtain had been pulled back to reveal an ugly scene.

★ ★ ★ ★ ★ ★

Freddie hardly slept that night. For years she had worried about her indiscreet talks with Janine during their drinking days. Janine knew enough to hurt her, used that as a tool to extract money from her. Maybe "extort" was a better word for it. Freddie's trip to New York had confirmed her rising suspicions that Janine was not who she pretended to be. She was a liar and a thief. But maybe even worse for Freddie, she was a woman who could not be trusted with a secret. If only Freddie could remember exactly what she had divulged during those tipsy hours years ago. Much as she would have liked to oust Janine from the house and fire her from her job, Freddie feared the unknown – the information that Janine had on her. A malicious woman could be a dangerous enemy and Freddie wasn't sure what her next step should be.

Unfortunately, Neil was in Canada on a job. Perhaps he could suggest a way to deal with Janine. But no, he would probably only say, "Fire her," and that was not possible. At least one worry had been lifted from her mind: her stalker, Lindstrom, Patrick's look-alike, had left town, according to Tim. What a relief – but for how long? she wondered

She tried to appear normal when she and Janine met in the kitchen for breakfast. Neither spoke much. Some of the tension of the past days remained.

"I think I'll go over to see Don Bailey this morning," Freddie said as she put another English muffin in the toaster. She watched Janine's expression for any sign of anxiety. Could she be worried about any possible change in Freddie's will? Her face showed nothing. Actually, Freddie simply needed to discuss some legal matters about her share of the leases in the shopping mall. She merely wanted to increase Janine's unease. Changing the will would not alter the situation: Janine would still be firmly rooted in the house.

How could one oust her? Perhaps she should confront her about her so-called "mother" in New York. And then what? There would be counter accusations. Freddie, "the well-known author," would be exposed as fraudulent, and even more threatening, Janine could start rumors about the "mysterious death" of Alberta Eliot. Al had been swiftly cremated, and the case labeled as "death by natural causes," but Janine's insinuations would be ruinous. It wouldn't take a great leap of faith for people to believe that Al's death was somehow brought about by her "insanely jealous" older sister. Freddie shuddered at these thoughts.

The telephone rang. Janine answered it. "It was Donald's secretary. Could you postpone your appointment until next week?"

"Fine," Freddie answered. "In that case I'll go over to the animal shelter and look for a playmate for Oreo. A tiny, snow-white kitten would be fun, wouldn't it?"

"By the way, don't count on me for dinner. I may be in New Haven with my cousin," Janine called after her.

* * * * * *

An hour later Janine answered another phone call. It too, was very disturbing. She was still upset when she met Jim Bankson at the Newfield Diner for their mid-morning coffee break.

"I could use something stronger than coffee this morning," she said. "My nerves are shot. Freddie's been prowling in her checkbook. I think she suspects what's going on in New York. Yesterday she went into the city, presumably to visit a sick friend. This morning I had a call from Grazio, the super in the building. He told me that a woman wanted to look at the apartment. He'd already told her that 'Mrs. Sherman was away in nursing home' but I guess Freddie didn't buy that. She wanted to look at the place. Said she was in real estate. Her name was Jenks, he said. He took her card and let her into the apartment. I asked him what the woman looked like. 'Tall, with plenty of red hair,' he said."

"Good God. Freddie must have had a card from Leslie Jenks to show him. Probably bribed the dago to get inside." Bankson put down his coffee cup and stared hard at Janine. There was silence – then he said, "The game's up, girl."

"And that's not all," Janine added. "Before that, I'd answered an earlier call that made me nervous. It was from Bailey's law office. Freddie's appointment's been postponed till next week. Gave my stomach a twist. I have a horrible feeling Freddie's going to change her will. Meanwhile, she's gone off to the animal shelter to look for another kitten. Guess she's hatching plans to leave her millions to some needy cats and dogs," she said bitterly.

Jim Bankson put down the paper napkin that he'd been using to mop his forehead.

"What are your plans, lady? You have exactly seven days to get yourself out of this mess. Think you can do it? It'll take more than a miracle. But I forget. You're a cool one." He looked at her, one eyebrow raised.

Janine did indeed have a plan. But first she had some calls to make.

47

The Long Awaited Call

Since her undercover New York visit Freddie had been too stunned to make any further moves about changing her will. She spent most of her time avoiding Janine as much as possible. In a few days she would be discussing her problems with Donald Bailey. He would best advise her how to handle the situation. Meanwhile she stayed out of the house, contacted old friends, made lunch and dinner appointments – anything to avoid a confrontation with Janine.

Late one afternoon, three days before her meeting with Bailey, an unexpected telephone call turned her mood from grim to exalted. At first she failed to recognize the caller – it had been such a long time since she had heard the slightly husky sound of Patrick's voice.

"Freddie, is it you? It's Patrick. It was good to hear from you, and I should've answered you long ago. Really rude, I know, and I'm sorry. I'm in Hartford now on business and wondered if I could stop by in an hour or so?"

Light-headed with elation, Freddie quickly ran up to her room and checked herself in her full-length mirror. There was no time to change clothes, but she was happy that she'd gone to the hairdresser's the day before and had a manicure as well. With a minimum of effort, a tiny bit of rouge, a smidgen of lipstick, and at the end, a wet finger passed over her eyebrows, she managed to look far younger than her 43 years.

Downstairs, she put fresh towels in the powder room and set out a bucket filled with ice on the bar in the den. Some water, whiskey and glasses were already at hand on the tray. Too bad there was no time to fix some fancy hors d'oeuvres. Oh well, cheese and crackers would have to do. Quickly, she hurried around the front room and the den, plumping cushions and whisking a dust cloth over the tables. Perspiration was threatening to spoil her hair and makeup, so she grabbed a Kleenex from the powder room to mop her face. Her mascara wasn't picture perfect, but it was too late to fix it. This isn't a beauty contest she told herself. Could it be called a confrontation? No, an absolution might be a better word.

Short of breath and with a fast-beating pulse she seated herself on a chair near the front door as she awaited Patrick's arrival.

48

Patrick's Return

While Freddie was preparing for Patrick's visit, Tim Dorrance was making his daily check on the grounds and house of Eliot Farm. Freddie's stalker was reputed to be out of town, but Tim did not relax his vigil. Long experience had taught him never to take anything for granted. Truth to tell, Tim did not have much faith in the Newfield Police Department to protect anyone. Ten years ago – not long after Alberta Eliot's sudden death – he had been fired from the police force. He had quarreled with his superior, contending that the investigation had been entirely too casual and cursory. Al, whom he had known since she was a child, had been far too young and healthy to die in such a manner, but her sister had resisted the idea of an autopsy and in Newfield what Freddie wanted, Freddie usually got. The cremation, at Freddie's request, had been swiftly carried out. The death certificate said the cause was heart failure, but Tim had remained unconvinced.

The sky was darkening and a mist was rising from the ground as he made his third tour around the property. Dimly he could see a tall, slightly stooped figure appearing at the entrance of the driveway. There was something about the man's height and the way his head was thrust forward when he walked that put Tim's brain on the alert. If it really was Lindstrom, Freddie's stalker, he had been smart enough to leave his Mercedes out of sight. From that distance and in the growing darkness it was impossible to positively identify the man. Whoever he was, friend or enemy, it was Tim's job to protect Freddie from harm.

"Guess I'd better stick around," he told himself.

At the sound of the doorbell Freddie jumped. She had been waiting to hear the approach of a car up the driveway. Suddenly she saw his silhouette through the glass of the front door. For one frightening moment she thought it was the stalker, Denis Lindstrom. The resemblance to Patrick was amazing, but when he stepped into the room she saw that this man was not Lindstrom. Though older, grayer, and a bit heavier, Patrick Nelson was still a very attractive man.

"I can't believe it's you," she cried as she took both of his hands into hers. "And to think that I was giving Janine a hard time for not mailing that letter. She's in New York today. I'm sorry you won't have a chance see her."

In her excitement at seeing Patrick again she had almost forgotten her recent discovery of Janine's deception about her mother. For the moment her anger at Janine was overcome by her feeling of joy.

He looked around the living room. "The place is as attractive as ever. The same Delft plates over the mantle. The same silly plant growing out of the spittoon."

Freddie laughed. "Remember, we have to keep a souvenir of the cigar era. That long-leafed tobacco built many fortunes in the valley. But we didn't get together to talk about tobacco. Let's go into the den and talk about ourselves."

She led him into the next room. "This room is almost exactly as it was when you last saw it – with one important difference. We added French doors that open onto a small, brick terrace. The plantings around it make it a cozy, private place for our afternoon tea. Somehow that old front porch had too many memories."

As she spoke she opened one of the doors and left it slightly ajar. "It's a mild evening. Might as well let in some fresh air."

She pointed to the bar. "As you may remember, I'm not much of a drinker, but this occasion calls for a celebration. Would you mind being the bartender?"

"Would a Scotch and water do?" he asked.

"Absolutely. But keep it light. There's so much I want to learn about you. Did you ever remarry? How are your sons doing? Is Chicago as great as they say it is?"

For the next hour they talked and drank, talked and drank as they sat on the couch together. He seemed to be doing most of the talking as he topped off her drink from time to time. After her second Scotch Freddie's mind had begun to grow fuzzy. She had so wanted their meeting to be an opportunity to heal old wounds, a chance for mutual forgiveness. Instead they talked like strangers. They traded banalities about careers, politics, even the weather. The teahouse days and Al were never mentioned.

Memories are usually rehashed at true reunions. Their memories of their first meeting in the art class, and their subsequent romance were not even mentioned. Do you remember, Freddie thought, those nights we spent together in my parents' heirloom bed? Or those nights you spent with my sister in New York? The Scotch was beginning to make her feel light-headed. This was her time to speak frankly with Patrick, to redress old hurts, but she was afraid to speak too much. She had already done too much of it with Janine.

"Here, let me top this off for you." Patrick leaned towards her and poured more Scotch into her glass. He noticed that

Freddie's words were starting to slur and that her expression had grown slacker. Freddie as a drinker had a new personality, a vulnerable one. For once he felt dominant and liked the feeling.

Now *he* was asking the questions, steering the conversation. "How much do you know about Janine?" He really knew the answer. For the past six months he and Janine had communicated regularly and secretly. She had been an important part of his past in Hartford. Janine had been named in the divorce action against him years ago.

He did not wait for Freddie's reply, but watched her expression as he said, "You may not know a lot about Janine's past, but she knows a lot about yours. Like those books you were supposed to have written."

Freddie did not notice the new sharpness and sarcasm in his voice. She did not respond. In her muddled mind she was desperately trying to say the words that she had so often rehearsed – "I'm sorry, Patrick, for denying Al her chance to be with you." Instead she drunkenly muttered. "I'm sorry, so, so sorry. Can't think too well now. Better lie down."

He stood up from his place next to her on the couch. "Sure, dear. Put your feet up and rest awhile. This cushion under your head will make you more comfortable," he said as he moved a cushion from the couch and placed it under her reclining head.

For a few minutes he sat in a chair nearby, watching carefully as she began to sink into sleep. Then he got up and moved back to the couch, gingerly withdrawing the cushion from beneath her head. She did not rouse, so much to the good he thought as he gripped the soft cushion with both hands and was carefully lowering it onto her face . . .

Suddenly, Freddie came to, opened her eyes and screamed a drunken scream – "Patrick! No! Don't do it!"

Patrick pushed the cushion down on her face and held it with all his might, while he used his right leg to kneel on her and pin her thrashing body to the couch.

49

The Eavesdropper

Freddie was still writhing and probably didn't hear the "whump!" of the body blow – immediately followed by a loud "Oof!" The cushion fell from Freddie's face and she screamed, "Help!"

She didn't know it just then, but help indeed had arrived. A second later she saw that Patrick was lying on the floor, making some kind of moaning noise, sweat dripping from his forehead. Standing over him – gun in hand – was Tim.

It seems that ever-suspicious Tim had been eavesdropping on their conversation from behind a shrub just outside the open French door. At the sound of Freddie's scream he jumped up, ran across the patio, through the open door and then delivered the best kick of his entire life, lifting Patrick right off the couch!

Before Patrick could gather his wits, Tim shouted, "Don't make a move, pal!"

He ordered Patrick to stay flat on the floor and put his hands behind his back, whereupon Tim snapped a pair of cuffs on his wrists.

Tim then looked over at Freddie, who was sitting trance-like in a semi-upright position. The shock of Patrick's attempt to kill her and the effects of the alcohol had left her too dazed to speak.

"Honey, are you all right? Tim's here. Now I've got the bastard and the police are on the way. They'll want to hear your story. That'll be tough, I know, but I'm here to help. I saw the whole thing."

Tim wanted to put his arms around her to comfort her, but he was too busy covering Patrick with his gun. Freddie lay back on the couch again, eyes closed as if to block out the memory of Patrick's attack. Occasionally a low moan came from her half parted lips.

"You bastard," Tim muttered through clenched teeth. His gun was right up against Patrick's neck. "Almost got away with it, didn't you? In the old days they'd have drawn and quartered you for this."

A wailing siren announced the arrival of the police. Two officers, guns at the ready, ran into the room. For a moment they had mistaken him for Lindstrom until Tim said, "This guy's not the stalker. He's an old friend of Freddie's. Would you believe they were having a kind of reunion? He tried to knock her out with some Scotch, then tried to smother her. Thank God I was able to stop him in time."

The larger of the two officers snarled at Patrick as he hauled him to his feet, "You are under arrest for the attempted murder of Fredrika Eliot. You have the right to remain silent. Anything you say can and will be used against you in a court of law. You have the right to speak to an attorney, and to have an attorney present during any questioning. If you cannot afford a lawyer, one will be provided for you at government expense."

After the cop had read the Miranda warning to Patrick he remained silent as the officers pushed him into the squad car. In his rage at being caught he curled back his lips and bared his teeth like a trapped animal. Tim gently helped Fredrika into his car. As she sat in the front seat on the way to the police station, Fredrika's whole body was shaking so violently that she almost fell to the floor.

"Why," she kept crying out, "Why me?"

"That's for us to find out," Tim said grimly. He drove at half speed until they reached the police station.

50

Fingering Janine

The police doctor was on hand when they arrived. Obviously, Freddie was in no condition to be questioned. With Tim and the doctor supporting her, she was led into a small room, which had a couch, a shelf of first aid needs and a water cooler. The doctor had already prepared a syringe filled with a very mild sedative. He had been told that Freddie had been drinking and he prepared the injection accordingly. Freddie accepted the injection without protest. Once she was settled on the couch, Tim left her. He was anxious to make his report to the police.

"Do you live alone? Is there someone who could stay with you tonight?" the doctor asked Freddie after she began to show signs of recovery.

Freddie's shaking had stopped and her mind had cleared somewhat, but her answer was blurry. "Someone? Well, yes. I have an assistant, Janine. Janine Something. Can't think of her name. Don't want her anyhow. Don't trust her. Try Donald. Donald Bailey." She closed her eyes and dropped off to sleep.

Fortunately, the police had sufficient details from Tim's statement, so their questioning of Freddie had been brief. Donald Bailey arrived within an hour. Freddie was still too traumatized to give him a real embrace, but he could tell from the look in her eyes that his kindness was appreciated. He and his wife had offered their house as a temporary refuge.

Bailey had long disliked and distrusted Janine, but had liked Patrick Nelson. To think that this attractive, intelligent man was now in a holding cell being grilled by the police – it was unbelievable. There was a rumor at the station that he'd fingered Janine in the plot.

Later, as he walked out with his arm around Freddie, Bailey whispered to an officer, "Is it true about her assistant being involved?"

As a lawyer, he knew that such a question was out of bounds. The officer, however, was a good friend. "Yes, but keep it under your hat. We've just put out a warrant for her arrest."

✶ ✶ ✶ ✶ ✶ ✶

The news about Janine did not shock Tim Dorrance. With his policeman's instinct he had always felt a certain distrust of the woman. Granted that she was attractive in a feline way, she was not, in his mind, a "straight shooter." He had felt this ten years ago, at the time of Alberta Eliot's death. She, like Freddie, had been very anxious to avoid a coroner's inquest.

She had begged him, "For Freddie's sake, can we get this over as fast as possible? She adored her sister. Couldn't stand the idea of someone cutting up her body."

At the time he had questioned her sincerity. Why was it, he mused, that some folks have an aura of honesty – Freddie, for example? This woman seemed truthful; she looked you right in the eye. Yet there was something intangible about her personality, something that made you wonder about her. He had heard the usual gossip about her lesbianism and the stories about her dominance over the younger woman, but he discounted those. He had also heard about her help with the elderly at Christmas and about the gala outings that she organized for minority children.

He also heard that Janine would inherit a nice piece of change at Freddie's death. Reason enough to want her dead. Freddie was only 43 years old. Under normal circumstances it would be years before Janine would see any real money and Freddie could live longer than Janine – she was a few years younger, after all. It had been rumored that Patrick had once been Freddie's fiancé. At the time of Alberta's death he had been living in Chicago and was not considered a suspect. Come to think of it, nobody was. Over Tim's objections the case was closed and Tim was fired from the Newfield Police Department. He had had the audacity to question his superiors.

Tim had to smile when he thought about his present standing with the police. Now that he was the hero who had thwarted a murder, his former fellow officers all but fawned on him. Perhaps they would re-instate him on the force? He pictured his response, "Sorry, guys. I'm doing pretty well on my own."

His thoughts kept returning to Janine and her connection with Patrick. If she had been in cahoots with him in planning Freddie's murder, as Patrick insisted, there was a good chance that she might have had a hand in Alberta's death, possibly to concentrate all of the Eliot fortune in one person – Freddie. Greed. Murder. Janine might be pure evil. Unfortunately, no case could be made in Alberta's death. The quick cremation had put an end to that. Her involvement in the present case would be more easily believed if it could be shown that she had had something to do with the death of Alberta.

The more he pondered, the more he became convinced of Janine's guilt. Until recently he hadn't seen her much over the years. After he had been hired by Freddie to protect her from the stalking activities of Denis Lindstrom, he had encountered Janine a few times.

He recalled his latest contact with her. He had come to the kitchen door to collect his weekly retainer. Freddie usually paid him in cash and invited him in for cake and coffee. Recently, Freddie had been away so he was disappointed to find only Janine at home. No coffee or cake was offered, and no cash.

"Sorry, but I'll have to give you a check," Janine said, as she sat down at the desk in the kitchen and wrote out the check. As she handed it to him he noticed a strong perfume, an odor that lingered on it after he put it into his wallet. When he got home he removed the check. The scent from it brought to mind a similar sickly-sweet hand and face cream once used by his ex-wife, Estelle. The stuff was called "Caress." He'd always remember those nights when she'd slather her face and hands with it before retiring. Her pillow would stink of it.

At the time of Alberta's death he had noticed the same overpowering scent on the cushion under her head. It was "Caress." Unwittingly, he had punned to his fellow officer, "There's something about this case that smells."

With that memory fresh in his mind, Tim immediately called one of his old buddies on the force and told him about Janine's possible connection to Alberta's death.

✶ ✶ ✶ ✶ ✶ ✶

Tim had hoped to see Freddie the next morning. There was no escape, however, from the avalanche of reporters and TV cameras. His initial pleasure at being in the spotlight soon changed to exasperation. What inane questions these people asked: "How did you feel when you saw the would-be-killer about to attack?" "How does it feel to be called a hero? "Is it true that you were once fired from the police department?"

It was an hour before he was able to get away from them. Unfortunately, when he arrived at the Bailey house to see Freddie, he found her surrounded by the same group of inquisitors. Things grew even more chaotic as some cameramen insisted on getting shots of "Freddie and her savior."

When it was over Freddie and Tim sat down for a peaceful brunch with Donald and Agnes Bailey. "Now I know what celebrities go through," Freddie laughed. "Imagine their gall. Insisting that I kiss Tim!

The telephone rang as they talked. Agnes handed the phone to Freddie. "It's some man. He sounded really upset."

Neil had just seen her and Tim on the TV. "My God. Talk about narrow escapes. Tell Tim I'll kiss him, too. I'll be down as soon as I can. Keep calm, darling. That bitch is going to get the full treatment when they find out how conniving she is."

Freddie agreed that Janine was evil. It was difficult and hurtful to believe that Patrick was evil, too. She knew that the pair had known each other in the past. Why would they want to kill her? she asked. Was it for money?

"I've never considered myself a rich woman," she told them. "As you know, Don, I've always been naïve about finances."

Her lawyer laughed. "That, dear, is the understatement of the month. Look how you trusted Janine. Look how she pulled off that con about her ailing mother. Incidentally, Tim, it would be a good idea to check out the mysterious Linda Sherman. See if she's really in a nursing home. She might actually be dead. Or she might never have existed. Well, when the case comes to trial we'll learn a lot more about the dirty doings of Miss Janine Fulton."

51

The Trial

Donald Bailey was right. Five months later, when the trial began, Neil and Freddie sat in the front row. Those who saw them together, happily holding hands, would not have guessed that the couple was witnessing the unveiling of a murderess.

"Mr. Nelson and Ms. Fulton did not start out as murderers," Walter Allison, the prosecutor, told the jury in his closing statement. "They had met many years ago in Hartford when both worked in the stock brokerage of Banks & Bedford. Alfred Eliot had a sizable account with them. He had been a shrewd investor, it seems. When Mr. Nelson met Fredrika Eliot some years later he remembered her father having a substantial portfolio and knew that it must have passed on to his two daughters. It was Mr. Nelson who urged Fredrika Eliot to hire Ms. Fulton. Both Alberta Eliot and her sister were targets for murder. Whether Alberta was killed in the same manner as was attempted on her sister we will never know, thanks to the quick cremation of her body. Mr. Dorrance's recollection of a certain odor of hand cream at the scene of Alberta's death – hand cream that only Ms. Fulton used among those who lived in that house – was compelling, but not conclusive circumstantial evidence that Ms. Fulton was involved in Alberta's death. However – as you heard from the testimony of the New York detective – we also learned that Ms. Fulton's mother, Linda Sherman, who died seven months ago after a mere two weeks in a nursing home, died of suffocation, a fact only discovered after her body was exhumed at the request of my office.

"We are not here to try Ms. Fulton for the murder of her mother – or for any involvement with the death of Alberta Eliot, but the circumstances of those events establish a pattern and tie in with the evidence and testimony of our present case, the attempted murder of Fredrika Eliot," he said.

The closing argument by Mr. Allison went on for almost an hour and then the jury had the case to consider.

After the eyewitness testimony of Freddie and Tim as to Patrick's role in the attempted murder, his own testimony implicating Janine and the exposure of Janine's questionable history and her current dealings, it did not take the jury long to find both of them guilty.

※ ※ ※ ※ ※ ※

Freddie and Neil strolled out of the courthouse together, arms around each other's shoulders.

Freddie suddenly stopped walking. "You know what? I just realized – I never did get around to putting Janine in my will!"

The End